ABOUT THE AUTHOR

Kellie M Cox is an Australian writer indulging her love of fiction and prose. With qualifications in psychology, she relishes writing about the human condition and the vulnerability of the psyche. A therapist, clinical trainer, creative coach and conservationist, she enjoys a dream life on the beautiful Gold Coast.

Wanting to see a change in the narrative of gender roles in storytelling, Kellie has created her publishing and production enterprise, Strong Female Protagonists and encourages others to write and produce work that challenges our preconceived ideas of societal values.

Most days Kellie can be found working with artists in the creative industries or writing her novels. When not writing, Kellie will most likely be saturating her social media accounts with photos of her adorable dogs.

Follow Kellie on social media as KellieCoxWriter and KellieMCox.

www.kelliemcox.com
www.strongfemaleprotagonists.com

WRITTEN BY KELLIE M COX

Fiction
Murderous Intent (2019)
The Last First Kiss (2020)
The List (2020)
The Reef (2020)

Short Stories
Death by Trident (2018)
Short Yarns for Big Imaginations, GCWA.

Murderous
Intent

KELLIE M COX

 Strong Female Protagonists

Murderous Intent

Published by Kellie M Cox
and

Strong Female Protagonists

www.KellieMCox.com
www.StrongFemaleProtagonists.com

ISBN 978 0 6484767 0 2 (paperback)
ISBN 978 0 6484767 1 9 (ebook)
Author - Kellie M Cox
Cover Photo - Blair Renwick
Cover Design - Blair Renwick
Logo and Website Design – Connor Renwick

DEDICATION

To my beautiful children, who inspire me to do better and to be better.
I love you more than it is possible to love.

&

My heart, my soul, my inspiration, Mark Simmons.
A little bit of your sparkle is in everything I write.

ONE

I know he is going to kill me.

It is three o'clock on a chilly spring morning. I could walk around the house checking the doors are locked to no avail. He will not be that obvious but he will find a way to enter. I can't remember the exact details of the nightmare that woke me this day, although the words I heard in my dream tell me everything I need to know. *He is close.*

He may not be inside the house, he may be just metres away. He is nearby and he won't stop until my eyes are closed, the last stains of my breath have touched my lips, and my body is limp and exhausted. He will marvel at his handiwork. The fact that he accomplished the unimaginable – that he finally ended my life.

He was close tonight, somehow confirming the exact location of my latest hideaway. He may have been just outside checking entry and exit points. Possibly even inside the house standing over me, watching me rest, his murderous intent the sole reason for my rude awakening from the latest instalment of visions of terror in my dreams.

He is nearby and narrowing in on his target.

I rise from my bed, and splash my face with water to freshen my red eyes, then crawl back onto the mattress, shaking. The warm covers do nothing to stop my body from convulsing as the tears roll down my face. No comfort will hinder the flow now as I realise the enormity of the message sent to me in my slumber.

He will find me. He will not give up. He needs to hurt me to feel complete. He will kill me. The last face I will ever see will be his, and there is no one in the world that can prevent this from happening.

It scares me to realise how comfortable I have become with the storyline for the ending of my life. I speak of it with ease, and try to warn those close to me so as to prevent harm to them if they bear witness in any way to the actions that destroy me. But in the end, I know it will come down to him and I. He will want to clamp his hands around my throat to feel skin on skin as he inflicts his sadistic pain on my soul. He will stare intently into my eyes as I lose consciousness. He will want to see the end to my life up close.

I know this because he has told me. He has explained to me how he will inflict pain on anyone who wrongs him. He describes in detail how he will butcher their body and dispose of them in pieces. The hate filled words trickle from his mouth as he speaks. His facial expression is void of the emotion necessary for the delivery of such harrowing content.

I can still feel his warm hands around my throat. They are a physical reminder of a possible end to my life so vivid in my sleep as to wake me screaming loudly into the night filled room. I imagine his slender but muscular frame standing beside the bed for just a brief second as my eyes open and adjust to the darkness. So real is the sensation that I endlessly repeat out loud between sobs, "he is here, he is here." I continue the repetition of these words over and over again. They ruminate in my head as if to desensitise me to their tormenting meaning.

He will kill me. I wait for the day. Not with joy, nor pleasure, nor even a sense of relief. Instead, I anticipate the day in the hope that I can maybe somehow change the course of events that he has planned with meticulous detail.

As my sobbing begins to reside, I take to my keyboard, choosing the words carefully as I try to remove the images from my head and translate them into a meaningful entanglement of thoughts and emotions. I cannot speak to anyone at this early hour of the morning, and even if I could, I would have no new words to share. This story hasn't unfolded in any extraordinary way to anyone else but me since I closed my eyes.

I retired to bed knowing I was a target of a vindictive man wanting to punish me for daring to challenge his world, and awoke with the instinctual sense that the punishment carefully constructed just for me will happen sooner than I had hoped.

It is now four in the morning, and there are few words on the screen. In between writing, the urge to check the doors is overwhelming. As I turn the handles to ensure they are locked, I know within myself that the few centimetres of timber and glass that stands as the barrier between him and I are meaningless.

He is already inside. Even if not physically, he is already inside my head. He is my greatest and only fear in the world. He will kill me. And at any point, my journey could come to an abrupt halt because he has chosen that exact moment to end my life.

I write my story not in the hope that it will save me, but in the hope that someone will recognise the truth and his crime will not go unpunished. I trust that one day he will be held accountable for accomplishing the unspeakable.

I release these words in an attempt to remove the images and thoughts from resonating further into my subconscious. I want to try to rest, but instead my brain is warning me to be cautious. To never feel comfortable. I can never forget that the end is not far away, and sleep for someone who has little time left is a luxury.

It concerns me at times the speed with which my story is unfolding. The plots to maim and dispose of my body perhaps not yet fully resonating with what may happen to one's soul under such violent undertakings. The schemes of my demise shared with those few people strong enough to hear the words and understand the intent but the true unspeakable terror is somewhat lost in the translation.

There is a noise under the house. I jump at the sound. My body is on high alert, and won't sleep again this night. I could check the doors once more, but know it is pointless.

I find a quiet spot in the library and continue to type the words onto the white screen in front of me, hoping that they will make the difference. I am huddled under my duvet on the couch. If I die, then what better place for it to happen than in this room in which thousands of words line the pages of old books. The stories inside holding hope, speaking of love and lives of great courage and strength.

If my stalker is downstairs or right outside the door, there is nothing I can do now to stop him. There is nobody who can reach me in time to prevent the inevitable. He knows this and has planned every second of his attack to take full advantage of the opportunity. He is trained for this and knows how to delve down into every last-minute detail in planning. He has thought about this for years. He will make this happen, and believes with every ounce of his being that he won't receive punishment for his crime.

He describes cutting me into little pieces with his chainsaw, wrapping the bloodied body parts into a tarp and transporting them by boat to a quiet location off the coast, saturating the waters with burley to attract enough sea life, then feeding my flesh to the sharks. He will find some way to believe it to be my destiny for my devotion to the ocean. For my love of marine life, I will someday become their meal. This will be the justification in the mind of a mad man.

The noises have silenced. He has gone, or at least for tonight. Should I try to sleep again? Is it best to rest for the battles that may ensue on daybreak? Instead, I stay alert, watching shadows come to life.

* * *

Dawn brings with it a spectacular sunrise, a beautiful reward perhaps for surviving yet another night. The number of sleepless nights left is unknown to me. it could be as little as one or decades worth. Only time will tell, a curious notion given that time can end at any second. The exhaustion of the battle is evident in my endless pursuit of counting down the hours.

In a moment, the sun has found its rightful place high on the horizon, shining brightly on the mountain range that frames my little piece of paradise, a writer's dream, a beautiful pole home set amongst high ranges, warm weather and beaches found nowhere else on the planet. I am here to spend my days writing my latest novel, a visitor for only a time, before again moving on, reluctant to stay put long enough to be found. The move from location to location takes its toll, though the positive is finally realising what is important in life. Carrying few possessions from one hideout to the next, it becomes apparent how little we humans need to survive, a laptop, a camera and a passport becoming the bare essentials for the travelling author.

Glancing at the time, calculating but a few hours' sleep, I climb from my warm covers in search of coffee, probably the most sought-after staple for any writer. Tapping away on the keyboard only a few minutes later, already energised by the first mouthful of the warm caffeinated brew, my mind wanders momentarily from the now automatic action of fingers lightly pounding the black and white keys beneath them.

Is it time to move on? My lungs grab at the influx of warm air inhaled at the thought of a move already. He is getting better at finding me. This time, it has only taken him six months. Six months and he is close, so close that I can feel him. I envision him in my mind. It has been years since I have seen him up close, a long time since I have been in near enough proximity to look straight into that tormented soul.

The name once so familiar to me is now just a two-syllable word I try to forget. Robert, the name of the man I was once married to. The name that once flowed from my mouth with loving regard now conjures only trepidation. I try not to utter it for I fear that saying the name out loud will produce the person back into my life. As if, by some magical force, merely uttering the sound of his name could bring the man who wants to kill me into my home.

My memory of his dark eyes void of humanity pierces through my consciousness. I feel him behind me, even if only in my imagination. The glistening sparkle of a kind soul absent from his dark brown, almost black irises. The sight of those eyes will remain etched in my memory forever. His thin lips barely covering the grimace that accompanies any thought of me. His temper always bubbling just below the surface of his skin, taking a mere second to erupt once provoked. The tensing of his muscles as a reaction to a perceived threat provides physical evidence of his intent to harm and not be harmed. Thoughts of destruction of property; of people; of reputations; of lives are the one constant in the mind of this maniac.

Never resting, always plotting. His thoughts are constantly going over and over in his mind, ebbing and flowing from one vengeful idea to the next. Once satisfied the plan has merit, the details are meticulously organised. This is his one superior skill, his attention to detail; his ability to plan every minute piece of a scheme, this is what makes him dangerous. Not his physical strength nor his intelligence, they are of mere mortal proportions, no greater than the average man or woman on the street. It is his ability to commit to a goal; to plan its every aspect and deliver with the precision of a surgeon, this is his most prized feature.

His arrogance that others won't be able to prosecute, that police so simple in their thinking won't be able to prove he did it. This is the confidence that pushes him to continue to search, to make his threats, and not give up until I am dead.

I speak aloud - a few simple words of motivation to myself. *Samara Sanders, you better keep typing. This book needs to be completed before you die.*

TWO

The waves break over the jagged rocks, crashing down and relentlessly shaping the foundations of the ocean floor as effortlessly over time as the sun setting each night. This beach is my spiritual home and the very reason for my settling in this location for a short while. Every few years, I need to feel the energy of this space and allow its magical powers of salt water and sand to recharge and heal the suffering of my tortured mind and body. I return to my home as often as I can. When here, I visit my spiritual place most mornings.

I step into the warm waters of the ocean, slowly making my way through the foam-capped waves that break one after the other against my tired body. I begin to feel energised again with each breaking wave. I search the horizon for the end to the set. It is within sight. I don't waste another moment, and delve beneath the surface of the next inviting rise of the sea. Plunging into the water I push through the oncoming strength of the current of the wave, eyes open to enjoy the rush of water around me on all sides. Feeling the majestic ocean flow over my body, I swim deeper into her waters. The white sand below me is soft to touch as I grab at it with my clenched hands. It grounds me.

I glance skyward to time my ascent through the waters to reach the surface following the latest break in the rhythmical arrangements of wave after wave. If the ocean felt fatigued, she never showed it, with her relentless pursuit of her deafening display of power. The warm water teases my skin. The smell ignites my senses. The tang of the salt tantalises my taste buds. The piercing heat of the sun on my face lets me know I am alive...for now.

I never feel scared when I am here, as if protected by a magical sphere. Nothing, and no one, can hurt me in my spiritual place. I find my favourite spot under a tree, feeling grateful that although many pass through, few people choose to stay beyond taking their postcard perfect photos to be the envy of their family and friends. I lay my towel out on the soft white sand and gasp a huge intake of the ocean air into my lungs. Closing my eyes, I feel my breath expand into my chest. Each fresh warm molecule of oxygen heals me a little more.

I feel the need to lay my head, but fear falling asleep. As if on cue, the Aboriginal elder, didgeridoo in hand, sashays across the soft white sand. He is heading for his place upon the large boulders that line the jagged coastline. I watch him perform his daily ritual as he climbs the rocks, effortlessly lifting his body higher and higher above the crashing ocean beneath him. His long legs find each foothold in this well-rehearsed routine, before finally settling in place, extended well above the sea in the most isolated piece of the shoreline.

He looks skyward as if saying a prayer. He closes his eyes and brings his mouth to the hollowed-out instrument, then blows on the mouthpiece. The heavenly sounds are muffled by the crashing of the massive waters on both sides beneath him. He lifts his majestic musical tool to the sky above him, and taps it twice on the hard rock at his crossed feet. With smooth slow movements, he repeats the act again. I have no idea what it all means, watching in awe at the peace and serenity of this ritual. A calm, washes over me as I take in the beauty and grace of the scene unfolding before me, and I feel not tired but relaxed. I am not arrogant enough to believe this performance is for me, but I allow myself to imagine for a minute that this spiritual man will keep me safe, even if just for the short while we spend together in our paradise.

Nowhere else but in Australia, in this quiet little piece of heaven on the Queensland coastline could a scene such as this unfold. In all my travels I have never found a place that holds as much natural beauty as my secret beach. I understand why this elder finds himself here day after day performing his ritual. This place just draws the soul in.

I slowly ease my back onto the towel below me, and relax my muscles into the soft sand. Feeling it manipulate beneath me to fill the contours of my body, I close my eyes and let the ocean breeze fill my lungs. Its healing powers slow my breathing and, as I close my eyes, I let my mind drift to the memory of the vision before me. I create in my mind the vision of the man performing his routine. I can barely make out the quiet sounds of the didgeridoo or at least I imagine I can. I concentrate on the waves crashing rhythmically against the shore, the occasional sound of an excited tourist but a background noise as I focus on the beauty of the nature around me.

I finally fall into a deep sleep. The long nights have taken a toll and my body can't fight the need for rest anymore.

* * *

"Excuse me." A male voice behind me rudely interrupts my dream state. "Wakey, wakey!"

The voice continues as my eyes try to adjust to the bright light reflected off the pure white sand. Not moving from my towel, I tilt my head back to take in the tall security guard. The man's black shirt and trouser combination is a stark contrast to the near naked attire of the regular beach goers. I barely utter a word in response before he informs me that I will need to move soon. I raise myself to my elbows and take in the numerous workers now scattered around my humble little campout. As I glance around, I see not one, but two whale carcasses. Made from fiberglass and wood, these sizeable structures have somehow been placed on the beach before me as I sleep. Film crews, all dressed in black, work quickly, laying coloured cables and yellow safety markers around the rocks and sand on all sides of me.

He speaks again. "They start filming here in a while, so you might want to pack up."

"How long have I been asleep?" I ask my new acquaintance.

He doesn't consult his watch. He obviously knows the answer. "I have watched you sleep for the last two hours."

I am embarrassed at my lack of awareness. I instinctively search the headland for the Aboriginal elder, the stranger I entrusted my safety to. He is long gone, the high protruding rock, his place of ritual, now void of any obvious life form. I wonder what he would make of the creative work being undertaken in his rightful home. I glance once more to the guard, assuring him I will move along so as not to disturb the business of film making around me anymore than I have. He wants to chat. His accent suggests he is American as he takes the time to tell me more about the filming yet to occur.

The fictitious whales take further shape, receiving a final coat of gloss to provide a wet effect on their smooth surface. The guard invites me to stay and watch the behind the scenes workings of a feature film and I instantly feel uneasy at the offer. I am keenly aware of my inability to decipher the hospitality offered by strangers. With my senses on high alert, I am hypersensitive to the dangers that can follow from a seemingly innocent exchange of words, and it becomes obvious to me that my lack of sleep in recent weeks has limited my ability to accurately filter for potential threats to my well-being.

I thank the guard for the offer to stay and begin to pack my towel and book, leaving just the tiniest amount of sand to travel with me in my bag. The feel of the sand on my skin and in my car on the return home keeps me grounded for the rest of the day.

I drive home wondering about the odd combination of comings and goings at my beach. The elder and his ritual providing within me a sense of calm in my soul; the deep blue waters bringing a renewed energy while the business of the movie set providing a welcome distraction and change of pace for the morning. I ponder the significance of it all, if there is indeed any to be found in it.

My mobile phone rings, and I glance momentarily to identify the name on the screen of the dashboard. It is Daniel, my new friend and fellow writer, one of those rare gems the traveller is sometimes fortunate enough to meet on social media; an experienced author looking to share, collaborate, and plot twist together. He has been persistent lately; eager to consolidate ideas for a new novel, and my first foray into the foreign world of co-authoring a manuscript is a welcome change for me to years of solo writing. I take the call, for I know that if I don't, he will continue ringing until I answer. He is on a self-propelled timeframe to complete the storyboard, and his energy levels are exhilarating, which has proven quite a nice distraction to long days writing alone on my deck.

"Hello there, darling!" he answers immediately. "Can I come around now? I have a great new character concept I need to get it down before I lose it."

He doesn't leave room for negotiation; his passion is as all-consuming and addictive as reading the beautiful words he puts to paper. You can taste his writing. It can be felt through every sense. I am in awe at the talent of this man. As much as a quiet day in front of the laptop is appealing, I recognise there is no room for refusal with Daniel when he gets this energised about an idea.

"Ok, but I am not home for another ten minutes," I inform him. I calculate the short drive home and add a few minutes for a quick change before he arrives.

"See you then, sweetheart. Oh, and Samara darling, you are going to love it. I am just telling you in advance so you can show the correct amount of enthusiasm as I share my brilliance with you."

I can't help but giggle at my friend and his exuberance of self-confidence. After he hangs up the phone, the drive home is uneventful, allowing me time to consider the next twist and turn of my own novel – a fiction thriller which is a new and untested genre for me, requested by some of my readers asking if I would consider venturing into something a little different for their reading pleasure. They have encouraged me to experiment with content a little darker and deadlier.

To suggest the different style of writing is out of my depth would be kind for I only know the world of long kisses, romantic gestures and Prince Charmings. This new venture is a risk for me, not only financially, but emotionally as well. I am acutely aware that I am being transported back into a world of murder and suspense that is touching on some very real and recent fears for me. I am not entirely sure I can finish my current piece of work, but am for the time being at least committed to trying.

As promised, Daniel is waiting in my driveway as I push the remote to drive into the secured garage. His face is radiating, and I can already tell today is going to be many long hours of writing and re-writing, plotting and storyboarding. He follows my vehicle into the garage and presses the internal button to allow the sliding door to close behind us. He is at my driver's side door as I turn to open the latch, and always the gentleman, has the door open and his hand outstretched to take mine in his as I swing my legs around to exit the car. He closes the door gently behind me, taking my large sand laden bag from my hands as he does.

"You are such a gentleman, Daniel. Why can't all men be as sweet as you?"

"Because my darling Samara. I am a one of a kind; unique; matchless; rare; distinctive; irreplaceable; exclusive; a rare gem; dare I say exceptional…"

"Yes, yes. I can't argue with any of that! But should we save this verbal genius for our creative writing?"

He smiles, clearly pleased with the use of the word genius. He pauses as he scans my face. "Oh, my dear, you are quite burnt. Where were you today?" he asks, knowing that my answer will always be the same. Guessing already from the tingling sensations to every pore of my skin, I know that I have been in the sun far too long. Falling asleep for hours obviously didn't assist with my sun protection plan for the day.

"So, where were you today?" Daniel asks again.

"At my secret beach, as always. I fell asleep on a movie set." I giggle softly to myself as I recall the embarrassment at being woken by the friendly security guard.

His face turns to one of concern. "You know how dangerous that is, my dear. Especially at the moment when you fear he is getting closer. You should be much more careful of your surroundings. What if he was watching you? What if he took that opportunity to do something?"

Daniel is one of the few people who knows the complete story of my relentless stalker. Being an author, an experienced traveller, and a man of reasonable maturity, I felt he could be someone who could handle hearing the details without the threat of traumatising him. I consider myself quite fortunate to have not only found a writing companion in Daniel, but a trusted friend who appears to care as much about my own safety as he would someone he had known years longer.

My silence spurs him on to continue his lecture. I have heard it all before and am not feeling quite rested enough today to hear again the perilous dangers that hunt me in every corner of my existence.

"Do you hear me?" he continues without encouragement.

"Yes." I relent. I want the sermon to end, but am mindful that he has my best interests at heart. "I will take your concerns on board." I say hoping that this will end the rant that I fear is continuing.

"Given your lapse in concentration today and lack of concern for your own safety, I think you should finally divulge to me where this secret spot is that you go to so often."

I smile as he pleads once again for me to share with him the details of the location of my secret beach. It is fast becoming better known to visitors, evidenced by the choice of location today for a feature film. I fear that my special little spot will one day be overrun with tourists, but until then, I am determined to keep its location a secret stored deep in my heart.

"You know I am not going to tell you," I inform him once more.

Any debate is fruitless. He knows that and relents quickly, changing the subject almost immediately to my latest project.

"And how is the thriller coming along? What is he up to now? Has he located her yet?"

I freeze at the surreal nature of this plot that Daniel speaks so carelessly about. It is not only a piece of fiction, but a reality playing out in my very own consciousness. "I don't want to talk about it at the moment, if that's ok?"

Daniel knows me well already. "Didn't sleep well, I take it my dear?"

"No, I have been awake since three am." I inform him. "I tried to go back to sleep but I couldn't so I wrote instead and then watched the sun rise."

Taking once more a mental scan of my face, he responds. "That, my dear, is why you fell asleep on the beach again today. You really must let me know where you are at all times. You know, in case something untoward happens to you." His words are meant to reassure me, but do nothing but increase the growing sense of dread in my stomach.

"Stop trying to force me to share my secret beach. It won't happen. You just need to go and find your own spot." I try to jest with him to lighten the seriousness of the moment. "Now, let's get started on this brilliant idea of yours, shall we?"

THREE

Night falls across the mountain range surrounding the poorly lit deck. I glance at the table smeared with cigarette ash, red wine stains, and mounds of hand scribbled notes. As predicted, the plotting goes long into the night, interrupted only by short breaks for food and refills of the endless supply of Shiraz, tonight's red wine of choice – the writer's other staple dietary requirement.

"I really need to stop smoking," I say out loud through the slightly raspy tones coming from my surprisingly tender throat. The combination of nicotine and alcohol has done nothing to support my latest attempt at improving the quality of my bohemian style unhealthy life choices. "And I need some sleep." I add with even more conviction.

"I am hearing it is time to take my leave." Daniel adds in his melodramatic fashion. He flounders as he rises to his feet. He is unsteady as he begins his search for his keys in the mess that lay on the table before us.

"You are not driving anywhere tonight. You have drunk far too much to drive. You can take the spare room. You know where it is," I instruct him.

"Thank you, my darling friend. I will do just that." He agrees without argument.

These long nights of collaborative creative inspiration are quickly becoming commonplace, and we have slotted into a nice routine of creating whilst building on each other's energies and ideas. Daniel proves his intensity for his craft, and being around another artistic soul provides much comfort for me.

Secretly, I feel instantly relieved knowing that I am not spending another night alone in my rented beach house. The nightmares have become a daily terror for me, and having someone close in the house, just a few rooms away down the hallway may provide me with some much-needed rest. Rest, which I should have retired to hours earlier.

I look once more to my fumbling companion. "Daniel, you must stop keeping me up late drinking and smoking with you. You are a terrible influence on me with these bad habits of yours."

Daniel turns momentarily, a wicked smile on his face. "Oh darling, you have no idea yet of what I am capable of making you do!"

I laugh at his harmless teasing and watch him head down the hallway and find with familiarity the way to the room he has begun to frequent as a regular houseguest. "Good night, Daniel."

"Good night, my precious. Sweet dreams."

"I hope," I mutter to myself under my breath.

* * *

The gift of a restful slumber, thanks to the addition of my guest in the spare room, works wonders, and I open my eyes well past my normal three am wake up to find the sun already high in the sky. I glance out at the mountains, their uneven green surfaces resembling a stunning combination of small-intertwined hedges. The majesty of the massive natural structures is deceiving in their solemn and silent impasse. I stare at the tiny white house set high on the hillside of the tallest erection, the dwelling's size massed by the enormous wall of soil and vegetation it stands on. Looking the size of a child's tree house, this dwelling would no doubt be a mansion of sorts. Dwarfed by its surrounds, it remains unimpressive from this distance.

I sit silently, listening for sounds of life from my houseguest. I imagine that he too is slow to rise after such a late night of artistic offerings. I begin to move from the bed to make us both a morning charge of caffeine, searching my room for something light to throw on. The heat of the day is already blasting through my open windows, the sunlight gently provoking my tender sunburn. I dress in my daily attire of bathers and shorts, imagining it would not be long before I plunge head first into the refreshing pool of my rented abode.

I tiptoe quietly from my room down the bamboo lined flooring of my hallway to reach the kitchen. I stop, stunned.

The white benches gleam with a shine I hadn't known them capable of, the bench tops are empty of debris from the previous night's attempts at culinary mastery. A large vase of frangipani stalks wafts a sweet scent through the room. The doors to the wide deck are open, allowing the breeze from the ocean side of the residence to filter through.

I feel slightly ashamed at my pathetic attempts at housekeeping, seeing how glamorous the kitchen is capable of looking. I feel even guiltier that I jump to the conclusion that because Daniel is gay, he is capable of such Martha Stewart-style décor and style. As much of a sweeping generalisation as it is to assume that all gay men can clean, cook and style, there really is no reasonable or plausible correlation for the connection.

I make my way outside to the calamity of the creative session completed just hours ago, expecting to find papers strewn across the dark timber of the table. The surface, once home to a myriad of artistic reasoning, houses just a single vase of freshly cut wild flowers. A small note is held centre stage on the sizeable outdoor setting. I walk toward it, eager to read its contents.

Dearest Samara,
Thank you again my darling for a wonderful evening. I hold much hope that our combined efforts will culminate in a bestselling Pulitzer Prize-winning spectacular. Rest up today, and don't do anything I wouldn't do. I am acutely aware that doesn't leave you many options, but what I mean, my sweet, is stay safe. Don't put yourself in any unnecessary danger again.
All my love, your dearest Daniel

I smile at the kind words of concern from my creative friend. It is surprising how quickly he has become so very important in my world. It is effortless to be around him, and comforting to know that someone cares so deeply for my wellbeing. He gives me a renewed sense of confidence that in fact the ending for my life when I allow myself to think of that dark place might not be guaranteed. Daniel somehow gives me hope that there might be a reasonable alternative than death by the hands of a mad man.

I unconsciously open the floodgate of memories that saturate my foremost thoughts. My recollection of the last face-to-face confrontation with my ex-husband is never really too far from my mind. I picture his evil smirk as I entered my tiny apartment in London to find him waiting for me; the smug arrogance that he displayed, knowing that he had found me after months of searching; his thinly veiled threats to end my life, with enough said to warn me of my impending doom without the necessary words spoken to allow a prosecution of stalking to prevail.

This meeting was years ago yet returns to my mind with ease and very real emotion. I close my eyes for a second to try to face my greatest fear. I muster all my strength to find the words I should have said to him that day. I look into the eyes of the madman, fuming with rage at my betrayal. Furious that I would choose to leave him behind in Australia and travel half way across the world just to be away from him. He swore that day that he would always find me, and I have never doubted it.

My eyelids fly open, startled by the sound of my garage door opening. The mechanical squeak is unmistakable as the most accessible and commonly used exit and entry to the residence.

I run back inside the house and grab my phone from the empty kitchen bench. I step quietly toward the entry to reach inside the large blue bowl housing my keys. My hand feels the empty tiled shell before my mind is able to register the significance of my dilemma.

The bowl is empty. My keys are gone.

I don't waste a second longer and make my way once more down the corridor toward my room. Knowing I can lock both my bedroom and bathroom door in an instant, I race toward my doorway. I resist the urge to dial for police help before I am safely behind the closed doors

My mind begins to scream at me. He is here! He is here! He has found me again. He is coming for me. My nightmares had been a forewarning of this exact moment. I find my way to the door in time to hear his footsteps coming up the stairs from the garage. He is close. He is not racing toward me. Why would he need to? He would be sure of himself. Certain of his plan for my end and he will not give in to the temptation to rush this pleasure he has been waiting so long to enact.

I slam the bedroom door shut and lock it behind me. I run to the bathroom and slide the door whilst I flick the frivolous lock closed. I momentarily chastise myself for not preparing for this moment with more precautions than a superficial lock on a door here or there, then look at my phone. The battery is low, but there's enough to make the one quick call to the emergency personnel that I need to save me. I press the numbers and hit the green button to begin my call. The sound of the ringing in my ear is smothered, by the banging of a fist on the bedroom door outside. I hold my breath and wait to hear his voice.

"Samara, my dear. Are you in there?"

The ringing ends as a female voice on the other end of the line asks professionally, "Fire, Police or Ambulance?"

I don't respond immediately, instead I listen for the male voice calling my name, followed by two more knocks on the door.

"Samara, are you ok? Open the door!"

I return my attention to the voice on the phone. "Hello, what service are you needing?" the operator asks me again.

"I'm sorry," I stammer. "I think I have made a mistake."

I hang up the phone, unlock the bathroom, slide the door open and make my way through the vacant bedroom.

"Daniel? Is that you?" I question through the closed door, needing to ensure I have indeed heard correctly before I dare to expose myself to the any potential threat that lies beyond.

"Samara, yes, it's me. Open up please! You are scaring me, my darling."

The concerned voice provides the comfort that I need to hear to know that I am out of danger. I open the door, and run into his strong arms. He holds me tight without saying a word, somehow knowing that I just need to feel safe once more. We embrace for some time. Neither of us feels the need to speak. We both understand that for a moment, my greatest fear had become my reality.

Finally, his sympathetic voice breaks through the silence. "Samara, my dear, maybe you need some more sleep."

I consider his suggestion for a second or two before introducing my own idea. "How about a champagne breakfast?" I ask with a hopeful tone. A small serving of liquid courage is exactly what I need right now to feel calm again. That, and possibly a cigarette to stop the shaking in my hands.

Daniel is all too willing to oblige, and offers to begin the brunch preparations whilst I pop the champagne. One worthwhile suggestion leads to another, and we decide to get an early morning start to our project, adding immediately to the ideas of the night before as we enjoy brunch on the deck. Daniel helps to ease my mind with a rational explanation of why he borrowed my keys from the bowl to do a quick trip down the road for some fresh bagels and juice. He explains that after writing the note, he checked on me whilst I was sleeping and decided to do something nice by surprising me with a home cooked breakfast spectacular.

I am thankful for his company. He has become a good friend, even if I feel more than slightly foolish for my stunning overreaction to a perfectly reasonable set of circumstances. We make good progress on the joint venture, and although at times I feel guilty for not working on my own draft, I am thankful for the distraction, particularly given my heightened sensitivity of late. I remind myself to talk to Daniel later about continuing the triggering content of my latest manuscript. I am keen to explore his thoughts on whether I should pursue this new genre given how it could possibly be the reason behind my recent terrifying nightmares.

Murderous Intent

FOUR

Another three am wake up from my nightmares, and I decide after a coffee and a quick dip in the pool that I am going to take my laptop and try writing from the beach. A change of scenery couldn't hurt, and it would feel good to be away from the house for a while.

I make my way to my secret beach with the plan to dive beneath the waves before I settle under my favourite tree to begin once more to put words on paper, or in this case, on the screen of my laptop.

Some of the main roadways are blocked. Signs indicate filming in progress and dictate where I can and can't park today. I make my way further up the hill to the scenic lookout perched high on the rocky outlet that protects the small beach from people passing by. I find a spot there, as fortunately it is still early, and only surfers and diehard beach goers have made the pilgrimage to the ocean so far this morning. I lock up the car, ensuring as I do that I have everything I need to spend a good few hours working on my manuscript. My towel, water bottle, phone, and laptop are all packed tightly into my expansive tote.

As I stroll down the wooden stairs that form part of the impressive walkway designed to protect the dunes, I am not surprised to find that the fictitious whales have taken up residence on the sand. Bright yellow indicator tape warns beach goers of the off-limits safe zone around the huge structures. I don't notice until my final few steps that someone new has taken my spot under my tree. It is the only real shaded area on the beach, and this stranger has made the space his own. He wears the same black t-shirt as the chatty security guard who woke me just days earlier.

The security officer is perched on a fold out chair, an icebox at his feet, his only saviour I imagine, from overheating on a hot day, and most likely filled with cold water and a homemade lunch. He smiles and says hello on my approach. I stop momentarily to take stock and find a new place to call home for a while. I can't help but feel slightly perplexed that my morning routine has been unsettled. I decide to head closer to the rocky outlet the Aboriginal elder visits. The protruding lower boulders offer some shelter near the water's edge, although I am sure it is a temporary reprieve until the sun moves in the sky in a few hours.

I place my bag and towel on a flat level part of the rock, and relieve myself of my unwanted clothes. As I stand taking in the horizon, the sun beaming down on the water, I am mesmerised by the relentless rhythm of the waves. The approach and retreat of wave after wave lapping the white sand continues without falter. I can't wait another second and run into the warm water to dive beneath her once more. The salt exhilarates my senses, my skin tingles and I let out my lung's capacity of air to watch the bubbles race to the surface as my soul fills once more with the energy of the ocean.

I return to find my bag and towel in place, but my space invaded now by not one, but two security guards. I rush over to enquire as to their intent. As I near the men, I recognise the chatty guard who woke me from my long nap on the sand days earlier. He looks unhappy, much unlike the pleasant and social being I had met not that long ago.

"Good morning," I begin as I approach them.

The chatty guard and his companion look at each other, acknowledging some hidden communication between them. They both stare back at me. Their frowns suggest something is terribly wrong.

"Are you the writer, Samara Sanders?" he asks me.

I can see now that he is glancing at his phone, then looking at me. He is obviously trying to place me from one of my social media posts, no doubt.

"I am," I reply, without delay. It is unclear to me why the unravelling of my identity would cause these two men to carry such worrisome expressions.

"Is there something wrong?" I grow concerned.

The chatty guard speaks once more. It is obvious now that he is, in some way, the other guard's superior. His face softens a little as he answers me. "It's just that you can't do that," he says, his tone is more of a plea than an instruction.

I feel confused as to what he is referring to. Is he suggesting that I can't swim here today? My mind boggles as to what I have done to warrant such attention. "I'm not sure what you mean," I say.

"You can't post that detail on social media. We just don't need this kind of attention. You will have to leave the beach now."

My mind races, and I wonder if he has me confused with someone else. I walk toward him, and instinctively take his phone from his hand to read the screen in front of us. My breath catches as I realise he is staring at my Twitter feed. A tweet from only thirty minutes earlier alerts my followers to our exact location. The words of the tweet are concise, but clearly encouraging the public to come to this very place to witness the latest Hollywood stars making a movie right here. I scroll up and down the page to see what else is around it, and see the tweet is being retweeted over and over again. It looks like my profile. In fact, it would appear that the message has come from my very own account.

I hand the phone back to the guard without saying a word, and reach into my large tote to find my own mobile. As the screen engages and I find the Twitter icon, I hold my breath again for a second, hoping for the best but fearing the worst. The blue screen takes forever to appear with hundreds of notifications that grow in number as I watch. My tweet is being retweeted both locally and around the world, with direct messages coming in thick and fast asking for more details on the secret location of the stars, and asking whom I had seen already and if people can get close enough to them for a selfie.

I place my hand over my mouth, and glance upward to the lookout above to see crowds of people starting to gather around; young people; old people; groups of happy smiling faces nattering away to each other, each with a phone or camera at the ready to catch a glimpse of a real-life celebrity.

I turn my attention back to the two security personnel. "I am so sorry." I say pleading with them for forgiveness. "I would never tell anyone about his place. I am so sorry. This wasn't me." I fall over my words as I beg for their understanding.

"Well it sure looks like your tweet" the quieter of the security guards, replies.

"I am so sorry. I don't know how this happened. I didn't do this. Please believe me," I beg them.

I sense that I am not going to get much further pleading my case with the onslaught of what could potentially be thousands of hopeful sightseers. I grab my bag and towel, and make a hasty retreat to my car. I place my sunglasses and hat on, throw my towel over my shoulders, and hope for the best as I try to plough through the emerging crowds. The heat and the noise combined becomes unbearable and the crowd thickens the closer I get to my car.

The vehicle is within sight, although it appears I may have a difficult time trying to drive out of this mess, I quicken my pace in a desperate effort to seek refuge behind the tinted windows of the four-wheel drive. I struggle in my bag to find my keys as I walk, not wanting to slow the pace at all I keep moving as my hand searches the depths of my bag until it finds the hard metal keys.

I take the last two steps to the car, and press the button to unlock the vehicle. I walk to the driver's side, and pull open the metal door that will soon be the protective barrier between me and what is quickly becoming a mob of excited movie buffs. The door swings open, and I step inside, closing it quickly behind me. I instinctively place the keys immediately in the ignition, and turn to throw my hold all onto the back seat. It is then that I see it.

My chest heaves and my stomach tightens as I take a moment to allow my brain to catch up with my body. The front passenger seat is covered in sand, which has been carefully placed with precision, with not a grain out of place, not even a particle on the floor of the car nor on the shiny new leather surrounds.

The sand is flat and even, spread with careful consideration and exact engineering. In the centre of the sand offering is the simple shape of a heart, enclosing a single beautiful shell. My chest is heaving. I feel short of air. I can't breathe. My face is hot. My body is heavy. A pain pulls at the base of my throat. I grab at the tugging of my heart muscle and clench it in my fingers trying desperately to stop this overwhelming feeling. I need to throw up and can feel the bile flooding my throat making its way to the back of my mouth. I open the car door just in time to retch on the hot bitumen surface of the car park.

I need to get air. I can't breathe inside the stuffy vehicle. I step onto the hard surface below, and grab at the aching in my chest once more. My arms are weak, overcome with the sensation of a thousand needles all piercing the skin at once. My head is spinning. I feel dizzy. I can't breathe. A muffled scream escapes my mouth, and I glance up to see the concerned faces surrounding me. A hand is on my arm. I try to make eye contact but I can't focus. A kind woman is trying to talk to me, and I can see the worry in her face, but I can't respond. I have no air in my lungs to speak the words to her.

"Breathe," I hear her say through the haze that fills my head. "Just breathe."

Her instruction to me is direct but gentle. I concentrate on her voice, and try to focus on her friendly face. I mirror her breathing, slow and steady, as I rise from my crouched position on the ground to stand. I know I need to control my breathing, to fill my lungs once more with the pure sea breeze. I will not pass out. I need to control this panic attack and not let it control me.

I quickly begin to feel normal again. The friendly stranger stays with me to make sure I am all right. I feel embarrassed, as the crowd formed around me begins to disappear down the hill to the film set below. I am ashamed of the mess I have left on the car park surface but feel unable to do much at this point to clean it away. Just as the fogginess of my mind begins to clear, I am reminded once more of the reason for my anxiety.

I turn around again to see the haunting sand message left for me in the front of my car. I glance to look into the back seat of the vehicle, an irrational response necessary for the time being to ease my sense of urgent unrest. I look around the crowd. He is here. I know he is here. My palms are moist, and I have to resist the urge to hold my breath. I dare not wait a moment longer. I jump back into my vehicle, quickly locking the doors behind me. I pull slowly out from between the white line markers indicating the allocated parking space.

As I take to the road, my eyes are glued to the rearview mirror. I know he will be following me. He must be watching me. I feel the urge to rebel - to stop my vehicle in the middle of the road, step out and scream into the vastness around me. Yelling at him. Telling him to go away. Letting him know that I can feel him close and I don't care. The intimidation, this is the hardest part. Knowing that something will happen. It always does, knowing that the when and where is at the sole discretion of just one person. I can't go home. Although I am certain he has found me already, I don't want to confirm for him where I am residing for the time being.

My rational mind tells me to drive straight to the police station. If he is watching, he will see I am serious about forcing him to leave me alone. I head for the main street of the sleepy beach side location, filled with cafes, bookstores, restaurants and surf shops. Little space is left for the seemingly unnecessary building that would house the emergency service workers.

I find a quiet spot, and pull over for a moment to check my phone. I make sure the doors are locked for what seems like the tenth time, and do a search for the nearest police station, hoping that I can convince them this time that the threats to my safety is not a work of my own creative fiction. It's a brief five-minute drive to the nearest location.

I take my time to constantly check to see if I am being followed. As I pull up outside the station, I make sure my phone is close by. I walk through the doors to an empty reception area, and the counter void of all human contact. Signs and posters around it offer promising advice, helpline numbers and alternate contacts in case of emergencies. I refuse to leave - this is an emergency. I have a madman trying to kill me, and he could be right outside the door waiting for just the opportunity.

"Hello!" I yell into the silent single level dwelling. "Hello, is anyone here?"

I hear shuffling of papers from behind a door, and the quiet murmuring of a human voice. Male perhaps? I resist the urge to yell out again. Instead I wait for the support I need to come to me. I hear the scraping of a chair on the office floor. The hard surface echoes the noises in the room behind the secured door. I can't force my way beyond. I need to remain patient. I need to help this person, whomever he or she is, to understand what is happening and offer some assistance in whatever way they can.

It feels like ages before I see the door begin to move. It is in reality only minutes. The male police officer, dark hair, stocky build, maybe thirty years of age exits the door. He appears distracted, still searching the words on the page in front of him. He finally takes time to look up at his latest visitor. "No one is here." He lets me know without yet facing me.

"Oh." I reply, not quite certain what his words means, given that he himself is present in the building, which would negate his statement. "I'm sorry, but I need some help. I am being followed." I add in hope of some form of sympathy from this person who has sworn his life to helping others.

He looks up. Obviously, something I have said interests him. He stares at me, then walks towards me and places his papers on the front counter of the reception area. He walks to the secured glass door, the last barrier between him and I. He unlocks it, not yet releasing me from his glare.

I take a step back. Uncertain if I have done something wrong or said something to offend this individual. His mannerism and sudden attention seem in clear contrast to his previous lack of concern for my plea for attention. I hope he can help me but feel uncertain about what more I should say or do in the moment.

He closes the door behind him and stands in front of me. He has not taken his eyes off me since his first glare. "You're that author, aren't you?" he questions me.

I am hesitant for a moment. His recognition could, at this stage, prove to be either a blessing or a curse. Or both.

"Um, I am a writer, yes." The statement reinforces everything that I hold true in my word. I may be able to write words, complete sentences even, but given a difficult situation, my ability to articulate anything verbally renders me speechless.

"You write romance novels," he continues. "I recognise your photo from the book. My wife reads all your books."

I relax for a moment. He hasn't recognised me from the unsolicited tweet from only a short time earlier, but instead from the headshot accompanying each of my novels. I am thankful for the fact that his wife buys my books, which hopefully might prove favourably for me as I try to gain credence with my unlikely story of terror that is yet to unfold. I thank him for recognising me, and ask if I can get some assistance. I don't want to appear rude or ungrateful, but I feel as if I have a very real situation unfolding before me, and need someone to take it seriously.

"How can I help you?" he asks, his concern for my wellbeing now evidenced in his facial expression and body language.

"I don't know where to start, but I have a stalker." Again, the words that I so desperately need to leave my mouth are nowhere to be found. I pause, trying to gain composure as I become aware of my inability to communicate the seriousness of this threat with due worth.

"Oh." He seems to gauge the situation immediately. "Is this like a celebrity stalking? A fan wanting to meet you or something?"

"Um, no. It's like an ex-husband who wants to kill me kind of stalker." I let the words sink in before I attempt to add further details. "He has just left me a message of sorts in my car." I pause again before I offer an idea. "Can you come and see for yourself?"

"I'm sorry. There has been an incident down at the beach on the film set, and I am the only one left here. I can't leave the building right now."

"Not even if I am about to get attacked?" I almost shout at him. I realise my mistake in attempting to elicit the right amount of empathy, and I apologise immediately. "I understand you can't leave. It's just that I am feeling really scared at the moment for my safety."

He sees my concern, and ushers me to the corner of the vacant reception area to take a seat. "OK then. Why don't you tell me what the note said?"

"The note?" I pause, realising how insane what I am about to say will appear to the officer. "Actually, there isn't a note as such. It was a message. A message in sand with a heart and a shell." The words have left my mouth before I am able to add the correct amount of description and inflection to cover the sinister nature of the act.

The next question the officer asks is the obvious one. "So how do you know who it is from?" he enquires, showing immense patience for the situation that deserves much better explanation than I can currently provide.

"I just know it is him. He has been stalking me for years, and I know he has found me again. I can feel it."

This last statement reaches the limits of the officer's patience, and he stands now to begin the steps to remove this particular crazy writer from his station. "OK, so I understand that you feel afraid at the moment that someone has left you a message. Do you think maybe it was a fan? A person who reads your books? A heart in sand doesn't sound to me like a threat. Do you think it might be a sign they liked your latest novel?"

He is hopeful, and in no way concerned for my safety with the same capacity I am. "By the way, would you have a book with you that you could sign for my wife? It would make her day."

I can see why he wouldn't be worried for me. This shouldn't make sense to anyone but me. I appreciate him hearing me out, and promise to bring a signed book back to the station as soon as I can. "Sergeant…" I begin to thank him for his courtesy.

"Just Thomas, will do."

I take a deep breath as I prepare to leave the safety of this small compound to head back once more to my rented vehicle sitting securely in the visitor's park of the fenced block. I say my farewells, thanking Thomas once more for his time before heading through the door and out into the bright sunlight to make the hasty retreat to my car. Once more I lock the doors. I look around and wonder what more I should do. I have nowhere else to turn. I can't go home for fear that Robert may be following me.

Back in the car, I look to the black screen of my dormant phone, and wonder what I should do next. On cue, the screen lights up and a familiar name appears before me.

I press the green button on the digital screen to accept the call from my car. "Hello Daniel." My very own knight-in-shining armour, or at least, I hope him to be.

"Hello, my scrumptious beauty. What are you doing today? Up for some more writing? I have a fabulous idea about how the two lovers meet. Do you want to hear it?" he asks with eager anticipation.

"I would love to." I agree, without hesitation. This is just the distraction I need right now, and the perfect excuse to not travel straight home, but instead to a safe and secure location with someone who will understand exactly the meaning behind the disturbing message in the sand. "Can I come to yours for something different?" I suggest to him. I am hopeful that he won't ask too many questions right now and instead he readily agrees to his home as the location for our creative collaboration today.

"Of course, my darling. I will open the red to let it breath in anticipation," he flirtatiously suggests.

"Daniel!" I begin by way of protest. "It is barely nine in the morning. Don't you think it is a little too early to be partaking of the red devil?" I jest with him.

I hear him snigger down the phone. He is careful with his next words so as not to offend his naive colleague. "My dear, we are writers. We must partake of whatever devilish desires our little hearts crave. It is what allows our artistic juices to flow."

I laugh out loud at his words. I am thankful for the light-hearted relief to what has already been an overwhelming start to the morning. "Thank you, Daniel, I will see you soon."

I turn on the engine of the car, and pull away from the safety of the station car park. I watch briefly for signs of my stalker, but soon relent. I feel too tired and too overwhelmed right now to even think of him. If today is the day that he decides to face me, his murderous intent flowing freely as he raises his hand to strike me, then I need to be prepared. Wasting energy searching for shadows isn't going to save me.

FIVE

I pull into the drive of Daniel's impressive beach house. The salt from the ocean breeze is barely able to make its mark on the floor to ceiling glass panelling before Daniel can be found outside cleaning it. I glance at my sandy feet and wonder if I should use the poolside shower before attempting to tarnish his impeccably clean Italian marble floor tiling.

I don't have time for any further hesitation before Daniel is out of the house and walking toward my car, a glass of red already in each hand. "Come on, sweetness. We have work to do."

His enthusiasm for his writing is intoxicating. He is swigging at what I assume is a full-bodied cabernet, waiting eagerly for me to finally step from my vehicle. I do so with reluctance, for I am still feeling a bit uneasy about the events of the morning and have not yet worked through in my head what details I should share with my friend and in what order.

I open the car door and take a step onto the perfectly paved driveway, and glance up into Daniel's smiling face. His welcoming grin turns immediately into a grimace as he looks deeply into my eyes.

"Oh my…"

He can't help but let the words fall from his mouth at the sight of me. I am aware that I don't look my best this morning, given the panic attack, the uncontrollable crying and the spontaneous fit of vomiting, and his words don't hurt. He is a kind friend, and part of me knows he is right. Being how he is, as always, Daniel will say and do whatever he wants without regret. I love his freedom to be himself without restraint from the perceived societal set restrictions to speech.

He thrusts the fuller of the two glasses into my hand. "Here, you need this more than me by the look of it!" he exclaims. He hesitates, maybe fully understanding for the first time that it is possible my morning hasn't gone as smoothly as his. "Do we need to talk about this?"

His sympathetic enquiry comes not a moment too soon, and I immediately begin to babble incoherently every last detail from my traumatic morning. He looks deeply into my eyes, trying desperately to piece together the ramblings of a mad woman. He takes another large gulp of the smooth red liquid, and finishes the remnants in one last mouthful. "I need another," he says, taking my hand in his and leading me to through door of his pristine home.

Settled onto the couch a few minutes later, all conversation has halted. Daniel has the bottle of red firmly grasped in his hand. Wondering if this is exactly what I need, I take a huge mouthful of red and also finish my glass. "Now, there's my girl!" He encourages me with genuine enthusiasm. He refills my glass, and makes it obvious he is now ready and able to hear the rest of my sad little story. "Go on…" He prompts me.

I fill him in on the details, my short visit to my secret beach, the hordes of movie lovers seeing what was meant to be my tweet giving away the seemingly hidden location to a big budget movie set, and finally, the message in the sand, my very public panic attack, and the quite useless appeal to police for assistance.

He sits stunned at the details unfolding before him. He tips the bottle once more to refill my glass again with the delicious red nectar of the gods. I have finished two glasses of red in quick succession, and immediately become aware of its effects.

"No, no more," I plead with him. My ability to plot anything succinct today is already in question, one more glass and I won't have the capacity for speech, let alone for writing.

"Shh, my dear. You have been through quite a morning, and you need something to calm you. Look at you. You are an absolute mess." He adds without care for the delicacy of my sanity at present.

I become even more aware of my current appearance, eyes red and blotchy from crying; sand and salt water still encrusted on my skin; breath embracing the not so subtle fragrance of bile from my stomach upset and hair still damp from my morning swim framing my face from all sides.

He reads my thoughts and finds a strand of hair stuck to my forehead by the salty adhesive. His finger finds the curl hardened by the ocean and releases it from against my skin. With a delicate touch, he moves the strand, and engages it softly behind my ear. His hand lingers near my face, and his eyes move to search the surrounding mess of curls. He strokes the long red strands with his fingers, ever so gently, and my eyes close just a little at the comforting touch of another human being. I realise for the first time how long it has been since I have let anybody get this close to me.

He has an idea and with that Daniel gets to his feet. "I know what you need. You need a massage."

Without waiting for reply, he has me also on my feet, and lifts my short, lightweight sundress over my head. He sits me back down on the couch, and makes his way behind me. His strong hands begin their work immediately, and I am drawn into a hypnotic state of calm within seconds. He kneads the tense muscles around my shoulders, working his magic. My mind starts to drift as I begin to feel more and more at ease.

I feel my body relax, and give way to the gentle persuasion of his warm hands against my skin. I am reminded momentarily that this state of calm actually exists. He lifts his palms from against my skin for just a moment, and his hands find the knot of my bikini top at the base of my neck. He takes just a second to pull at the elastic material releasing it from its fray and allows the string to fall forward. The dark blue triangular pieces of material covering my breasts come away with them, and my eyes flit open as my hands race to cover my nakedness.

He witnesses my display of discomfort, and urges me to relax. "What are you worried about? It's not like I haven't seen breasts before, my darling."

I release the breath I am holding in my lungs. My anxiety these days is never far from the surface, and I feel it first always in my breath. I am thankful for the vague reminder of Daniel's sexual orientation, and try to relax once more. Still covering my breasts, I feel awkward. Searching the soft luxurious furnishing around me to find a small scatter cushion, I pick it up and hold it to my chest.

I hear Daniel sigh a little, obviously tiring of my conservative response to life. Our opposing natures to the most mundane situations must wear on him. Daniel is as large as life, nothing ever appearing to bother him. Not a care in the world, except of course for his seemingly obsessive compulsion with cleanliness and order, the likes of which extend only as far as his house and self. His behaviour, in stark contrast is anything but ordered, his mannerisms flamboyant, his actions extravagant and often unbridled. For the most part, Daniel does and says, as he wants when he wants, the true artist living life full of passion and with no regret.

My mind races back to the couch as his hands move past my shoulders, down my chest, and towards my breasts. I try to clutch the cushion closer to stop the unanticipated invasion to the parts of my body not normally held by another person. He senses my discomfort, and once more dismisses my shyness.

"Shh, stop already. There is nothing to be embarrassed about with me." As he leans to speak softly in my ear, I feel his mouth close to my face, and the discomfort within me grows.

His breath is warm against my neck, when suddenly I feel his lips on my sensitive skin. His hands have now found their targets, and mold the soft, plump flesh of my breasts beneath them. His lips make contact and are moist against the spot beneath my ear. My skin tingles at his touch, and my body immediately responds to the pleasurable sensations. My mind is racing as I pull my head around to turn and face him. He lifts his mouth so that he faces me, and his eyes search for mine waiting for me to speak.

"But Daniel, I thought you were…" I hesitate to finish the sentence; not sure I completely understand how to formulate the thought without appearing rude and insensitive to his sexual orientation.

"You thought I was what?" He tries to ply the final words from me his upturned smile a suggestion that he already knows what I am trying to ask him.

"It's just I thought you were…gay." The words are finally out of my mouth. I wait for the response, hoping that I haven't said anything to offend my friend.

"Gay, straight, bi, pan…all labels, my dear."

He seems non-perplexed by my confusion, and ready and able to steer me clear of any misconceptions I might foster. He seems encouraged as he makes his way around the couch and to a sitting position beside me. The bare skin of his leg beneath the hem of his Armani shorts touches mine as he pushes up against me. He takes my face, his hand under my chin as he turns my glance to his, holding it just millimetres away from him as he continues to explain his philosophies of life to me.

"We are writers, my dear…artists!" he adds with flair of the dramatic. "We must feel what we feel, we must love who we love. This is how we write, my darling. We mustn't hold back, for in doing so, we may miss the opportunity to create something… extraordinary."

His words make sense to me, for it is this passion that he lives every day - this passion that first attracted me to his creative energy. I envy the ease with which his words of wisdom flow from his mouth. His spirit is contagious. He keeps his hand in place on my face, forcing me to endure the words, to consume them with my soul. His eyes lock onto me as his lips find my own.

It feels odd at first, this sensation of intimacy with another human being. I haven't been this close to anyone since Robert. I allow myself to fall further into this guilty pleasure as he moves his lips from my mouth to my neck, gently sweeping my salty hair from my shoulder. He finds the sensitive spot running from my shoulder to my ear, and the entire right side of my body erupts at the touch. My skin feels hypersensitive, and every touch, every kiss sends my senses into overdrive.

I am hesitant to follow his movements. Something holds me back. He is a confident and attentive lover, and has taken the lead, driven in his pursuit to explore my body with his mouth. Something - a feeling, a longing - is missing at present. The mechanics of the act are well rehearsed, the movements confident, but a part of me is finding it difficult to connect. I try to stop my mind from racing, for an artist must feel in order to create. I want to experience without thought or judgment, so force my mind to let go - to think of nothing, no one - as I close my eyes to allow my senses to take over once more.

He stands and presents his hand to me. I place mine in his, and lift my body from the couch. Without words, he walks me to his bedroom. This is a place I haven't seen before. It is neat, of course, and the décor is simple, yet masculine. A beige coloured duvet the staple of the colour palette for the room. He leads me to the bed and ushers for me to sit. The fabric beneath me is exquisite in its softness. He stands in front of me and begins to remove his clothes. I watch, unable to tear my eyes away from the sensual feast in front of me.

His hard body is revealed little by little, and I find myself smiling as I take in the sight of it. He is now naked in front of me, and I find my hands reaching out to feel his skin. He pulls me to a standing position once more as he begins to remove the last remaining item of my clothing. As my bikini bottom is dropped on the bedroom floor, I feel the anticipation build in me. There is no awkwardness between us. No words are spoken. There is no passion between us, but there is no fear either. I move onto the bed, watching him intently as I anticipate his next move. He walks slowly to the other side of the bed, and it is then I notice for the first time the tattoo on his right shoulder.

It is curious, but familiar. A yin and yang symbol of sorts, created using the shape of a wave instead of the traditional light and dark that it is known for. I smile in appreciation of the design. It is familiar in a strange kind of a way. Not entirely of course, but it is strikingly similar to one I had sketched years earlier. A sense of kinship flows through me. Maybe there is something more to this than what I had ever imagined. Two artists, two like minds, two friends with very similar values and thoughts. I regret for a moment, never going through with the original tattoo design for this would have been another talking point for us for some time.

I don't mention it at present, for words would drive me from this place of joyful anticipation. He is finally on the bed. He lays next to me, and stares deeply into my eyes. No words are needed. We are both sure and ready for what will happen next. He rolls over to kiss my lips once more as I close my eyes again, and allow my mouth to move with his.

It is hours later that I wake alone in Daniel's bed, the 2000 thread count sheets soft against my skin. I feel what I imagine to be minute particles of sand at the base of the bed, and can't imagine it to be too long before the sheets are ripped unceremoniously from the mattress to be replaced with untarnished virgin fresh clean sheets. I wonder for a moment where Daniel is, and lay quietly, listening for any clues as to his whereabouts. The house is quiet as I stretch, lifting my arms high above my head, pointing my toes and releasing a breath. I scan my body in an attempt to diagnose how I am feeling.

I feel energised, relaxed, but also alive. I'm a little proud of myself for going through with this unexpected session of daytime lovemaking, and I try not to let my mind begin the inevitable rundown of feelings and thoughts attached to such an action. I try to concentrate on staying in my body for the moment at least. I roll to the side of the bed, and find my bikini bottoms on the floor at my feet. Aware that my top was left on the couch outside, I drag the sheet from the bed to cover my modesty. I tiptoe from the room, and head down the cool white tiles to the lounge room.

Daniel doesn't see me at first. His head and full concentration are on the screen in front of him. A refilled glass of red on the table beside him, a cigarette hanging from his mouth as his hands work their magic on the keys in front of him. I know this sight well - this is Daniel in full writing force. Not to be disturbed, I turn slowly and quietly so as not to distract him.

"Are you feeling any better my dear?" Daniel's voice rings through the silence of the empty space between us.

I turn to face him again. I smile at the simple nature of the question. "Yes, thank you. I am feeling much better actually."

"Glad to have been of service," Daniel replies before returning to his screen.

The words sting a little as my pride takes a small puncture to its recently inflated ego. It's not that I imagined Daniel was falling in love with me. The romance writer in me hasn't depleted my intelligence enough to even allow such a suggestion. It's just that I never wanted anyone's pity sex. And as harsh as that sounds, it is exactly how I feel. Daniel is a loving and caring friend, and has demonstrated the depths of his loyalty by taking me into his bedroom as the ultimate act of kindness.

I look to thankfully see my clothes neatly folded in the arm of the chair in front of me. I grab them, and rush back to the bedroom to get dressed. I feel the need to leave as soon as humanly possible. I throw the discarded sheet back on the bed without fitting it onto the mattress, and make my way back to the lounge to search for my car keys.

Daniel looks up and asks the obvious question. "Are you leaving?"

"Yes," I stammer.

I don't want to appear unappreciative of his hospitality, but I need a little space on my own for a while. He stands to walk toward me, lifting from his desk my keys as he does. He places them in my palm, and wraps his arms around me, before placing his lips once more to mine for a gentle kiss.

I feel slightly confused by the gesture, but wholeheartedly grateful that Daniel has cared to show his affection again in such a way. It gives me some relief at the thought that our friendship hasn't been affected by what we allowed to transpire between us. As Daniel releases me from his embrace, I make my way to the front door. I turn to wave goodbye as I step into the car, start the engine and head for home.

SIX

My body leaps upright in bed, and my mind takes a second to catch up with the sudden drama unfolding. The noise from under the house forces me from my sleep. The sound is distinctive, for the pile of timbers crashing down would wake even my distant neighbour. I instinctively grab for my phone in the dark. With practiced precision, I check the time. It's three am. I sigh, admitting to myself that I already knew the answer to the question of time before even activating the screen on my phone.

I sit still listening for further sounds from under the house. It is a dark night, and I am barely able to make out even the outline of trees from the large windows that form the walls of my bedroom. I hope to see a glimmer of light perhaps, an indication that someone is using torchlight to see through the darkness beneath my floorboards.

I see nothing, and hear no further sounds. I wish I could fall back into the soft pillow beneath me and retire my imagination for the night. I think about heading down the stairs to search alone for the answer to the mystery noise this morning, but I do this often. With curious nervousness, I normally take to the night in search for some comfort, for some reasonable explanation to the sounds that stir. I know today is one of those times, and I reluctantly give up any further idea of sleep for the time being. Swinging my feet out of bed to find the soft floor beneath me, I reach for the torch on my phone. The red indicator signals it is on a dangerously low level of battery. I decide to leave it on charge and search the property by old-fashioned torchlight instead.

I flick the switch on the white bedside lamp to find the end of the charger with more light. The shade doesn't come on. I fumble in the dark and find the power lead. I place it in the end of the phone, waiting for the familiar tone of the alert to sound at the commencement of charge. It doesn't stir and I notice the phone isn't granted a top up of battery. I walk toward my bathroom. Finding the bathroom light, I flick the switch. Again nothing. I sigh, knowing that this requires some exploratory investigation of the power box to the side of the house. For a short while, the search for the mystery sound is halted as I throw on the clothes draped over the chair nearest the bed and step outside in the dark.

Just then, another noise captures my imagination, the distinct sound of gravel crunching underfoot. My hearing has become attuned to the different noises in the dark over time, with this one quite particular to this house. The gravel edging of the candy crush coloured pebbles that adorn the pavers at each side make quite the distinctive noise.

He is here. He has been getting closer. The message in the sand on the front seat of my car was evidence of that. He is here. The thought circles in my mind. Tonight, could be the night that he faces me. The night we may look into each other's eyes and stand face to face as my predetermined destiny plays out. I stop and think for a moment. I am not sure how to play the next hand dealt to me. Do I step forward into the darkness and meet him where he is, or do I wait it out until he comes inside to find me? No locks, no security screens, no alarms will withhold his entry now, for he would have planned for all of these. The certain sabotage to the electricity supply proves he has taken the first steps to enter the house as it stands in darkness.

I look around the room, unsure what I should do. Given so much time to think and prepare for this day, I still feel unready for it. Emotional exhaustion has clearly overcome me with the years of watching over my shoulder listening for every noise and anticipating this moment. I barely feel as if I have the energy to fight back. It is all but depleted. Maybe it is just time, possibly that I should stop fighting. Tonight, this will end one way or another. I take both my mobile phone and my torch and head for the door leading to the back deck. I know this area of the house the best as it leads to my office, my own sanctuary of the small wooden deck by the pool where I sit and write every day.

Making my way slowly and quietly down the stairs, unaided by the torch I hope to see for myself the shadow lurking in the darkness. As I hold my breath I descend the stairs. I am beyond scared. My muscles are tense as I begin to tremble with the fear of what will happen next. I wait for whatever is going to launch out of the night to grab me. It is so quiet now that I can hear my own breathing. All signs of life beyond the foot of the stairs are now silent. Robert and I play our game of cat and mouse as we both wait for the other person to make the first move.

A sudden loud noise from the side gate forces a scream from my mouth. It is a shriek that pierces the quiet of the night at this time of the early morning. Someone has jumped over the side gate for the sound of it is distinct. With newfound strength, I make it to the bottom of the stairs, race under the house, and to the black iron-gate that secures the right side of the pole home. The gate is vibrating, a result I imagine of someone's recent use of it as a hurdle to catapult over its sturdy frame. I have forgotten the keys, and then notice that the latch isn't secured. I push the gate, and with ease, it opens. I fumble with my torch to light the area beyond.

There is nothing. There is no one to be seen. No car is visible in the street outside the house. No movement, no sensor lights activating a warning of an intrusion. There is nothing to indicate the existence of human life in this dimly lit road in front of me. It's as if he is a ghost. Robert has disappeared into thin air once more. I stand in the silence of the night for a moment or two, allowing myself the time to calm my rattled nerves. This was the closest I have felt him for some time. I wonder why he ran.

As I return myself to the present moment and prepare to head back inside, I remember the issue with the electricity. I don't want to begin to imagine what catastrophic mess I will find in the metal box housing the electrical circuitry to the home. I venture to the left side path that snakes its way past the front gardens and to the poorly lit side of the home housing the specialist box. I am keenly aware that once I open the box I will have little idea of how to resolve any technical issues. Instead I hope that there is an obvious switch that needs flicking back on. I use the light of the torch to locate the large grey metal box and as I reach out to open it I find a new dilemma unfolding.

The normally easily accessible housing for the power switchboard has been padlocked. Not just locked, but a large round hole has been drilled in two places to secure a padlock almost the size of my fist. I gasp at the damage done to the property I have rented off my elderly landlord for just twelve months. I can't imagine she would have done this without giving me a key or at the very least, letting me know she had secured the area. It leaves no doubt in my mind that my ex-husband has damaged the box. Who else would do this and not inform me. It makes perfect sense. Control over the electrical access to the home would mean control over lights, power, alarms, even smoke detectors if they had inadequate battery supply.

I shiver in the cold night air as I imagine him standing in this very spot, plotting and planning to destroy me and taking the first initial steps by disarming the essential services that may attempt to keep me safe from harm. I am shocked at the audacity of my ex-husband. Coming to my home, damaging property, preventing me from accessing what for the time being belongs to me. The person with a mind who believes he can do these things and not be punished for it, is a person I do not want to contend with. A man who feels he is above the law, believing his own lies; manipulating people at will; truly so confident in his own ability and righteousness that he doesn't think he is doing anything he should be punished for - this is the mind of the madman that follows me around the world as a means to end my life.

I feel sick in my stomach. This time was far too close for comfort, and I feel the need to be inside again - to curl up under my duvet and pretend this nightmare isn't happening. I decide to wait until morning to contact my landlord, the warm-hearted Shirley, for I know she will be able to shed some light on whether or not she authorised a padlock to this box. Although if I am honest with myself, I feel with absolute confidence that she will know nothing about it.

I make my way back around the front of the house and through the iron-gate along the side path. I pull it closed and try to turn the key to secure it. It won't lock. The mechanism is moving but the gate won't fasten to the fence with the locking system. It is as if it is too short to hold in place. I jiggle the key and the gate a bit more hoping that it will surrender to me and find its place in the structure. After several more attempts I give up and decide to try again in the daylight. Everything always feels easier to do when the sun is shining and I have had a full night's sleep.

I head back up the stairs, making as much noise as I need for there is no longer the necessity to listen for whispers in the darkness. I know he was here, and feel certain he has left for the night. Well, at least, I can hope he won't return again this day. I heard him jump the fence. I couldn't see him anywhere outside the property. Whatever he was planning for me tonight was clearly disrupted by my appearance on the stairs.

My bare feet reach the upper deck, and I am aware of the hollow sound the wooden flooring makes under my step. This is the sound I hear often from my bed, the sound of footsteps against the hard surface. I often dismiss them. It has become hard to tell reality from fiction in the early hours of the morning. With my senses always on high alert ready to warn of impending danger, I have grown accustomed to every small essence of a sound that radiates through the darkness.

I close the glass sliding door behind me, and wipe my feet on the aqua blue mat that welcomes my return. Heading firstly to the kitchen, I find a tall glass and fill it from a glass bottle of filtered water from the state-of-the-art stainless-steel fridge, recently added for the comfort of new rental tenants. I take a long cold sip, and feel instantly refreshed by its hydration. I hope that the contents of my fridge are able to stay cool long enough to sustain their freshness while I resolve the issues with the power supply. I refill the glass, and turn to make my way back to my warm bed.

I pad along the bamboo floors to my bedroom door. Still in darkness, I use the torch again to find my bedside table, and leave the near full glass on the surface next to the welcoming mattress. The torchlight once more lights the way to the bathroom door.

I step inside, and as I scream into the emptiness, my hand releases the torch to let it fall on the smooth hard tiles beneath me. Banging and rolling along the ground, the light bounces off the wall, the sink and then the mirror, before finding a final resting place under the sink vanity unit.

Frozen, I stand, my hands covering my mouth to muffle my own scream. My legs feel heavy and unable to move from their spot, even though my mind tells me to run. The words on the mirror in thick red lettering, lathered messily as if in haste spell a simple message to me. *SLUT.*

I feel the anger in just these four simple letters. I sense something behind me, and turn to scream with fear into the night once more. I find nothing but an empty room. I face the mirror again, and as my eyes adjust to the darkness, I can see the outline. I fall to my knees, and search for the light source. I find it with ease, and stand to shine the torch on the eerie message to me.

The colour, the childlike scribble with which it is written all adds to the sinister nature of the intent behind the single word. My mind ushers back to earlier the day before, and my intimate encounter with Daniel. The surprising turn of events that found my writer friend and I in bed together. I can't help but wonder if this is the act the message is referring to.

I don't doubt that if Robert had been following me, he would have no second thoughts about watching me through the windows while at Daniel's house. Being on the beach, the house itself is open to the world, the large glass windows and doors barely ever hindered by curtains or drapes. Instead, the delicious view of the Pacific Ocean in all its glory is left evident for all to see. If my ex-husband was watching me, he would have seen the indiscretion that occurred - the indiscretion that was the momentary lapse in my normally sensible behaviour that found me in bed with a friend. I feel sick. My stomach instantly tightens, and I feel the need to throw up. My stomach as always is the first to indicate the seriousness of the unfolding events in front of me. I rush to the toilet, and lift the lid just in time to empty the contents of my stomach into the porcelain bowl.

I sit on the cold tiles for a moment, not sure if I will repeat the action. The muscles in my stomach are already tender from my upset the day earlier in the car park near the beach. I place my hand on my stomach, and hold it in place firmly. I am hot, the skin of my face flushed by the exertion to my stomach muscles as they heave once more. My breathing doesn't have time to falter, for which I am thankful. Changes to the rhythm and depth of my breath generally indicate the beginnings of a panic attack. The taste in my mouth is vile. I finally rise and stand at the basin, taking in large mouthfuls of water to refresh my tongue and mouth.

As I find my toothbrush and toothpaste, I begin the routine action of brushing my teeth. I want to cleanse away the taste of fear from my breath. I look into the mirror at the word taunting me as I move the brush around my mouth. The anger in me rises again at the use of the word, deemed antiquated in this day and age of women's rights. I feel mad beyond belief that he would even use such a term to describe a woman. Probably aware of my dislike and disdain for the term, he has chosen this to elicit an emotion in me that he knows will cause me to want to fight against him.

This taunting of me, this cat and mouse game of hide and seek he is playing is far more damaging to my psyche than a face-to-face confrontation, for it is always in the shadows that he waits for me, forcing me to move past my comfort zone, past the point that a sane person would want to move to join him in his evil twisted game of manipulation and fear. I want to grab at the nearest towel to wipe the filthy word from existence, but I know that I will need the evidence of his presence to press charges against him.

I rinse out my mouth, and decide to head back to bed to try to get a few hours of sleep before I am forced to pay another visit to the local police station. I hope that Sergeant Thomas is available again to hear the updates on yesterday's message in the sand. I try to set a reminder in my brain to take with me an autographed copy of my latest novel as a token of appreciation for his assistance. If I could indeed label his underwhelming inaction offered so far as assistance of any kind.

I head back to the bed, and instantly feel tired at the sight of the warm soft covers. I wish I could crawl up into the plumpness of the fabric and stay there forever. As I step closer, I lift my glass to my mouth to take one more sip of the cool liquid. My mouth touches the side of the thin glass as my lips press against a cool hard metal object in the water. I try to adjust my eyes to make it out in the dark. There is something in my glass.

As I place my two fingers inside the glass I feel my mobile phone between them, and lift it from the icy cold water. The realisation hits me hard - he is still here. He was inside the room with me as I sat on the bathroom floor. As I brushed my teeth, anger rising in me as I was forced to see the message on the mirror, he was here all along. I can't remember where I had left my mobile phone past the point of walking down the stairs with it. He must have been watching from the shadows the whole time, lurking there taking in my every move. He must have seen me place it down as I stood looking at the padlock on the power box or struggle to try to close the side gate. He must have waited in the shadows, close enough to touch me, close enough to reach his hand out at any time and destroy me.

My stomach turns to knots, and my breathing stops. My head is on fire with a searing heat that radiates from my face in my panicked state. My two arms, one holding the glass, the other the phone, spontaneously lose all strength and drop the items to the floor. I can't catch my breath again. I try to suck air into my lungs, but it does nothing except to cause a heavy sharp pain in my chest. I feel the familiar pins and needles, and the tingles of my arms. I can barely lift them to press against the throbbing in my chest. I throw up again, this time with no ability to make it to the bathroom. I collapse on the carpeted floor under my feet. I can't phone for an ambulance, for my mobile is lifeless. The screen of the mobile phone is black and unresponsive. The tones it should sound now silent from its imprisonment underwater. Resistant to but a mere splash of liquid, the total submergence of my phone has rendered it utterly useless.

I lay on the floor in a heap. I can't breathe and I can't scream.

Robert's presence is first sensed and then heard as he clears his throat. I turn on to my back to face him, acutely unaware of the hand reaching down for me. His soft leather shoes stop beside my head, his expression void of any emotion as he stares at me. My eyes widen, and I attempt to scream, but he is quick to place his hand over my mouth.

"Shh." He commands me to be quiet. I nod indicating that I have accepted his demand and will make no further noise. He removes his hand from my mouth.

"How have you been Mrs. Sanders?"

I am unsure how to respond to such a surreal question. I feel the floor beneath me vanish as I am left dangling in midair. His strong muscular arms pick me up and my feet are unable to find the floor. He is taller than I remember him to be. I'm not sure what is going to happen next. I don't know how to respond to his still unanswered question. I don't know in this moment in time how to fight back. He opens his mouth again. It is mere inches from my ear.

"Don't look so worried my wife. I'm not going to kill you today."

I blink long and hard for just a second. His words don't translate into anything tangible enough for my brain to process. This scene in the performance that is my life is happening so fast I can't keep up. I am yet to respond. I can't find words or actions to counter his surprise attack. My body, like the limp deer caught by its prey, is numb, hoping the pain will pass sooner and the end will come quickly without a fight. Still holding me, he brings my face closer to his. His cold, soulless lips touch my flushed cheek as he utters the final words I hear from him that day.

"Until then, my love."

He places me back on the ground. My legs cannot hold my weight, and I instantly drop to the floor. His next action is surprising. He takes the glass from the bedside table and places it to my lips. His unspoken intent is for me to sip the cool water. I take a mouthful and the refreshing liquid replenishes my dry mouth.

"Drink up, my wife. You look parched."

He holds the glass in place until I have finished every last drop. The blurriness that seeps through my mind renders any further argument or battle impossible. Without effort, he lifts me into my bed and pulls the covers over me. Whatever he has placed in my glass, the unknown substance he has forced me to drink takes holds. The response is quite immediate as I fall into the darkness that is my forced sleep.

SEVEN

When I wake, the sun is shining through my windows and the rainbow coloured lorikeets are at their food tray chirping loudly to let me know I am late to serve them their breakfast. The furious noise of the birds I have nicknamed, the superstars, is a sign that I need to rise like them to greet the early morning and start to write. It is the best time of the day for me to be creative, for the solitude and peace of my little beach retreat brings a harmonious routine to my days. I reach over to look at the time on my mobile phone. My eyes are blurry, my head slightly foggy as I search the blank frame for the illuminated digital figures that indicate the time of day.

I press the home key hoping that as I do, the memories of the night before that come flooding back are mere fragments of a bad dream. But as images and words replay in one continuous unconscious stream from my memory, I realise that I didn't imagine them. He was here.

Looking down, I see the bed sheets are neatly tucked in at the sides and corners. I am clothed in my thin black singlet top and panties. I spring upright in bed. I feel no pain. I don't believe I have been hurt. But he was here. He spoke to me. I remember his chilling words to me, his promise to not kill me, or at least for that night anyway. And the mirror, I remember the mirror in the bathroom, and secure my phone in my palm to run to find the words in red scribbled across the mirror.

But there is nothing. The mirror portrays back to me a tired looking, bleary eyed fiction writer set against the backdrop of a polished reflective surface. The word has disappeared. My mind is racing through the details of just hours before. The three am wake up; the noise under the house; the padlock on the electricity box; mobile phone in the glass of water; and the single red word defying me to fight back. I remember his hands picking me up from the floor. Then nothing. After his chilling words, my memories fail me, as I can't recall a single moment after that and before waking alone in my bed this morning.

A flick of the bathroom light switch brings an illumination to the room. This proves another indication that my imagination may have momentarily seduced the cognitive functioning of my brain. I glance down at my phone still refusing to ignite its normal array of functions for me. I remember the electricity box. I recall the padlock on the switchboard box and race toward the front door to find it.

I check that the doors are still locked. As I open them, I wonder for a brief second if I should not have touched them, instead leaving them as evidence for police who will no doubt want to fingerprint my entire home. I turn right after the front door to meet the path to the electricity box. The padlock is gone. I had expected as much. But fortunately, the large freshly drilled hole is still evidence of his sabotage. I stop for a moment and open the box. There are no further clues to his presence. Everything looks in place, not that I would actually know for sure.

I close the door to the large metal box and drop my head as I calculate the pieces of evidence that I have to share with police. All I have is one neatly drilled hole in a metal box and a mobile phone that won't turn on. I feel defeated already at the conversation that will follow the barrage of questions that will surely amount to nothing at all. I have been through this process before, several times before. The police on previous occasions have been unable or unwilling to offer anything more than mere suggestions. They will suggest more security or cameras in the home and videoing any evidence of his presence. All great ideas if we are dealing with your standard stalker, but this man, he doesn't do the obvious. His actions are subtle. He knows what he is doing. Well-practiced already. He has been following me for some time.

I decide to head to the police station rather than try to call them to my home. I imagine they might be less receptive to my theories if they have to make the early morning trip themselves. I throw on some clothes, grab my car keys and head for the door. It almost seems redundant to lock it, but I do anyway. I drive straight to the station, wishing I had my partner in writing with me to support me through the questioning. If only I had some way to reach Daniel. I don't want to arrive on his doorstep at this hour of the morning. We might be familiar, but there are limits to any friendship. Still, some strange sense of pulling someone else into the trenches with me would provide me at least a slither of companionship and normalcy.

There is no way I can go to his house on the journey to the station. Daniel is most likely sleeping off a red wine and cocaine-induced flurry of writing. As I arrive at the station, I step from my vehicle and take a deep breath as I hope for the best but imagine the worst. As good fortune has it, Sergeant Thomas is on duty again and looks happy to see me. Thankfully, I have remembered the copy of the book for his wife and promise him I will retrieve it from the car. He escorts me past the front reception desk and into the large open area of office pods to sit me down and listen to my story.

I begin to tell him the story of the intruder during the night, my ex-husband Robert. I notice he isn't writing much. He hasn't asked to record my statement either. Both of these factors are not positive signs that my concern is going to be actioned today. He has but a few pertinent questions.

"Did anyone else see him?"

"Did you record the conversation?"

"Did you take a photo of the writing on the mirror as proof?"

All good questions, none of which I can answer with a positive response in my favour. I feel as if I am banging my head against the wall, and discouraged by the lack of concern my night of terror conjures up in the friendly but ineffective officer.

"Woohoo!"

A lighthearted greeting sings out across the open space, coming from the front reception area. I recognise the familiar voice immediately and so does my companion. Thomas stands and yells back across the wide space. "Daniel, I won't be a minute, take a seat."

Daniel looks directly to me through the clear glass reception area. "What are you doing here my dear?" he asks with a hint of concern in his voice.

Thomas looks to Daniel and then to me. "You two know each other?" he asks with obvious surprise in his voice.

Speechless, I just nod in the affirmative. I am surprised to see Daniel here, and wonder what he could possibly be doing at the police station so early in the morning.

"Can I come in? You look like you need a hug darling." Daniel asks pleading for entry. I am guessing he can see my obvious distress. There would be only one reason for me being here, and Daniel appears quick to make the correct assumptions as to the purpose of my visit.

Sergeant Thomas gets to his feet and walks toward the front reception door to allow Daniel to enter. My friend rushes toward me and wraps me in a strong embrace as soon as he reaches me. "Oh, my dear. Had a scary night, did we?"

Daniel's words confuse me. "A scary night?" I repeat back to him. "Daniel, he was in my house!" My voice rises as I say the words out loud once more. "Does no one here seem to understand what I am saying?" I pause for effect, and with desperation for confirmation that I am not going insane right here in the police station. "Daniel, please tell him. Tell him about my stalker."

Daniel's words sting as they make their way to my brain. "Your husband?"

"Daniel!" I shout straight back to him. "He is my ex-husband. Does no one understand me?" I shake my head. I begin to feel dizzy, and try to stay in the moment before the onset of another panic attack begins. I turn to the Sergeant once more for one final attempt to beg him for understanding. "The writing on the mirror; the damage to my mobile phone; the padlock on the electricity box. He was there in my house. He threatened to kill me!" I scream at him.

Daniel once more pipes up. "What padlock on the electricity box?" For some reason, he finds this one point the most interesting out of everything I have listed.

I respond with a tone of exhaustion at my lack of progress. "There is a hole in the metal frame of the electricity box. Last night there was a padlock on it and now it is gone, but the drilled hole is still there. He switched off my power last night before he came into the house."

"Switching your power off and then back on again is not an offence." Sergeant Thomas is quick to dismiss my concerns.

"Samara, my dear. There is no padlock on the power box yet." Daniel throws his observations into the mix.

"No, I know there isn't now, but there was last night and there is still a hole in the frame that he drilled where the padlock was."

"Do you have a photo of it?" The Sergeant is quick to ask. Obviously still searching for any evidence that could prove my accusations.

"No! I told you my phone is dead. He made sure of that by drowning it in a glass of water."

Daniel speaks again. I feel more than frustrated at his constant interruptions. He certainly isn't helping my case at all. "Samara, I drilled the hole into the electricity box for you." This new piece of information takes some time to filter through the appropriate cognitive processes to make sense to me.

"What?" I am rendered speechless at this new piece of information.

"Yes, I thought I told you. I spoke to Shirley, your landlord and told her about your stalker fears and asked if I could padlock the electricity box for you. She thought it was a good idea and said she would consider upgrading to a proper monitored alarm system for you as well, seeing as you always appear scared about living alone. She is a dear old love that one." Daniel smiles as he adds the final piece of seemingly useless information.

I stand staring at my friend in front of me. I search my memory for any fragment of recognition of a conversation about a padlock with him and can't remember a word of it. I let out a deep breath and sigh once more as I drop down in defeat into the hard, plastic chair beneath me.

"I just haven't got around to buying the actual lock yet. But of course, my dear, you will most certainly have a key, along with Shirley. It just means that no one can ever tamper with the electricity which it seems is a concern for you for some reason." Daniel completes the mystery with his final piece of information.

Thomas seems satisfied that the case is closed. Not that he seemed to have taken me seriously at all to begin with, but he is now obvious in his intent to rid us both from his workplace. He turns first to Daniel. "Would you be able to take her home mate? She seems to be a bit lost at the moment." Daniel nods as acceptance of his willingness to comply. Thomas leans down and places his hand on my shoulder. "Can I suggest you go home and get some rest, Mrs. Sanders?"

"It is Samara," I say, letting him know that I do not want to be referred to by my married name any more than I already have to for professional purposes.

His words are of little comfort for rest is the last thing I need right now. I need someone to take me seriously, to listen and understand and hear the very real threat to my life that I am facing alone. Sergeant Thomas looks into my eyes for some sign that I will at least consider his suggestion. I don't reply, and my silence is space for yet more infinite wisdom to leave his mouth.

"And maybe you should go back to writing romance. Writing a fiction thriller seems to have gotten to you. Maybe it's making you a little more paranoid than you might typically be." Thomas says.

I look into his warm eyes. He really is speaking from the heart as he tries to console me. I am too exhausted to get mad at his lack of motivation to act on my behalf. How can I, given that the evidence placed in front of him was flimsy at best? And with Daniel's input, any shred of integrity I walked in with was quickly spirited away. I find it hard to believe that I have forgotten an entire conversation about placing a padlock on my power box as a security measure. There is even less chance of remembering words around a security system. I thank the Sergeant for his time again and begin to make my way to the door.

"Hey, could I get that book for my wife by any chance?" Thomas asks with gentle persuasion.

"Yes of course, I will get it from the car."

My voice is monotonous and flat. I leave Daniel inside as I walk slowly to the vehicle to retrieve the copy of my latest romance fiction for Thomas's wife. I can't recall what he said her name was, so take the copy and a pen back into the station to sign it in front of him. I make it just a few steps inside the station again, when I sense I have interrupted something. The hushed whispers between the two men halt as I enter the room. That awkward feeling of walking into something I shouldn't have ensues.

Both men turn to me, their conversation now completely ended as I join them. It is quite obvious from the expressions on their faces that they did not want me to hear the dialogue between them. I wonder if I may have been the topic of conversation, but don't say so out loud for risk of appearing even more paranoid than they both obviously think I already am.

As I am keen to get going, I sign the novel for Thomas and leave it with him. Daniel walks me to the door and out to my car.

"What was that all about?" I ask, eager to find out what the hushed tones could be hiding. I figure I have more chance of finding out information from Daniel without Thomas around.

"Oh, it's nothing," Daniel says, quick to dismiss my suspicions. He very clearly does not want to engage in this conversation with me. I feel his pace increase as his need to get to the car becomes quite obvious.

"It's not nothing Daniel!" I challenge him. "The two of you stopped talking the moment I entered the room. What were you saying?" I sense my friend hiding something, and need to know if it has someone to do with my stalker.

Daniel looks embarrassed, an emotion I have never seen in him before. "It's just my dear…" He pauses as he considers his next words carefully. "The friendly Sergeant has helped me out with a few favours recently. The police in this station are known to have the purest supply of cocaine around." He blushes, seemingly shy about revealing the source of his illegal drug supply.

The confession explains a lot behind the obvious lack of regard for public safety from our local police Sergeant. His senior position in this small town offers Thomas the ability for a sideline income from commercial drug distribution that his public servant salary would struggle to match. I feel deflated at the realisation that the person entrusted with ensuring the longevity of my life is more interested in securing his financial wellbeing with illegal and highly corruptible endeavours than investigating threats to my life. I berate myself silently for allowing my trusted friend into this unhelpful situation. His presence did nothing but to increase Thomas's already waning interest in my theories for the demise of my existence.

I feel the tension in my stomach rise through my chest and land firmly in my throat. My anxiety is growing each day, and seems to erupt with little cause now. I place the palm of my hand on my stomach in an attempt to control my breathing through deep breaths into my diaphragm. Daniel looks at me with obvious concern, and with good reason. My unexplained visions in the night and increasing panic attacks must have him wondering what sort of person he has got himself entangled with. Finding it hard to locate words whilst at the same time concentrate on my breathing, I simply raise my hand to indicate my need for a moment's pause to the current discussion.

I want to be mad at Daniel. I want to yell at him for the frivolous nature in which he handled yet another one of my dramas. But it is impossible to be angry with him when I look into his eyes and see his growing concern for me. Just as my breathing begins to settle, I hear from the entrance to the station behind me, the familiar voice of Sergeant Thomas. His footsteps weighty, made possible by the police department sanctioned heavy-duty boots. He begins to speak, but stops when he sees the disorganised state of my physical being.

"Is she OK?" he asks Daniel.

"She does this sometimes, but she'll be fine," Daniel replies.

Lacking the morals and integrity to resist lining pockets with the profits from highly dangerous drugs is one thing, but being a government appointed emergency worker, trained in first aid, and offering absolutely no physical or emotional support to a member of the public when in need is an entirely different matter. I want to reach out and slap their heads together, but for some strange reason, I can't. I feel a certain kind of empathy toward the two men before me for neither appears to have any idea of how to assist me. They stand in front of me, Thomas, with his hands in his pockets. Daniel, one hand resting gently on his hip, the other running fingers through the crest of his dark hair. Both men looking directly at me, entirely unsure of what to say or do next.

I sense a smile form on my face and a slight giggle replaces the fist of panic caught in my throat just moments earlier. I remove my hand from my stomach and let the laughter fall from my mouth. The men first look to me and then to each other. They smile and join me in frivolity. The relief in their faces is obvious, as they both appear to be able to manage laughter much better than the provision of emotional support. The tension between the three of us disappears.

"Samara," Sergeant Thomas begins to address me this time. "I have just had an idea that might make you feel better."

I am listening. I had hoped for a little more action-orientated solution than a plan to make me feel better, but at this stage I am open to any ideas that are forthcoming. "What did you have in mind?" I enquire hopefully. Keen to hear from him.

"A friend of mine, a self-defense guru is back in town, contracted by the film studio to act as stunt coordinator on set. I think he would be happy to run through some moves with you." He pauses, reflective in a thought that has caught his attention for a moment. "It would be my way of saying thanks for the book." He smiles at me as if searching for some form of acceptance of his offer. I wonder why he has had the sudden change of heart and increased interest in my safety.

I really have no valid reason to say no, so accept the offer of assistance. In reality, I probably won't be staying around long enough to even meet this friend, so I have no hesitation in agreeing. As Thomas already has my email, he lets me know he will pass it on, and have his friend contact me whenever he is next available.

We say our goodbyes, and I am happy once more to be alone with Daniel. I want to make him understand that my stalker was in my house, but I don't know what more I can say to make him believe me.

He speaks first. "Samara..." He pauses to make sure I am listening, my thoughts quite obviously elsewhere. "My dear, why don't you come back to the beach house? I will make you some food, and we can put on some music and forget all about this stalker nonsense."

Again, there it is - that patronising tone with which every man I know is treating the threat to my life. Even more reason, I conclude, for leaving this part of the world as soon as I can. The time has come once more to plan out my next trip and new home for a short while. The move has come about a little sooner than I had hoped, but my agenda is no longer my own to set. Before getting down to planning my next destination, some good food and company would refresh my weary soul. I agree to following Daniel home, and spending some time relaxing in a safe space. Following my overnight ordeal, a little avoidance can sometimes be the best strategy.

EIGHT

Daniel's midnight blue Porsche pulls into his pristine driveway just seconds before I do. The door of the garage is already opening, and I see Daniel's hand motion me to follow him in. He pulls his car to the left, leaving ample space for even the less skilled of drivers to manoeuvre a vehicle next to him. I shake my head, and let him know I will park in my normal spot on the drive. I see the brake lights of the parked luxury vehicle disappear, and Daniel is out of the car in an instant walking toward me.

"Park in the garage," he orders me, as if I didn't fully comprehend the hand gesture to instruct me in the same.

"I'm fine, I'll just leave it here as normal."

Daniel has my driver's side door open with incredible pace. "Come on, out you get, my darling."

Arguing with Daniel is fruitless in the end, so I relinquish my vehicle and stand aside as I watch him masterfully position the car in the secured housing. He is parked and ready to close the massive door to the area before I have even managed to move more than a few feet from where I alighted the vehicle.

"Come on, my sweet."

He encourages me to find some speed to my movement, but I feel like every step and every thought at the moment is wound up in a dreamlike state. Not quite real, but not imagined either. I find my feet and walk toward my extremely controlling friend.

"Why do I have to park in the garage today?" I demand, wanting to know why Daniel is now choreographing every detail of my day.

"You have a stalker, my dear." Daniel doesn't soften the facts for anyone. "If your car is off the street, no one will know you are here. It is for your own safety, my precious girl."

I relinquish my combative attitude, as I understand that my faithful friend just has my best interests at heart. I feel thankful that he can be so practical in these moments when my head is not thinking straight.

Walking up through the gorgeous beach house is always a treat. Continually adorned with fresh flowers and the smell of coffee lingering in the air from the first brew of the day, the white tiled floors are always immaculate with never a scrap of dust or sand to be found. A near impossible feat, I would have imagined, for someone living on the white sands of this wondrous paradise we find ourselves in.

Daniel marches straight to the kitchen. "You are in luck, my dear. I have a fresh chilled bottle of my own coffee blend this morning."

"Oh, coffee." The words fall from my lips like honey. The sweet murmuring of that one word anticipates the heavenly first mouthful of this special stimulating brew. "I'll have mine black."

"Yes, admirable, my dear. As all good coffee should be taken. Pure as God intended." He smiles at me as if, for the first time today, I have actually said or done something that pleases him. "But this morning, my dear, is espresso martini time." His devilish grin rises and his white teeth glisten as he stares in my direction, seemingly waiting for a response to his teasing.

I giggle a little at the thought of starting my day on espresso martinis, and silently hope Daniel is jesting. I continue to look on as he gathers the ingredients from his bar - the shaker, the strainer and two martini glasses. As suspected, he is serious about a boozy morning at the beach house.

"Daniel, maybe I should just stick with coffee, if that's OK. I don't want to get into the habit of drinking so early in the day."

A roar of laughter fills the room. Daniel is momentarily halted from his actions, placing the crystal glasses to the bench as his head falls back, his gorgeous face contorted in the act of hilarity. The mirth controls him as he doubles over, his shoulders now slumping toward the ground before him, as he appears unable to contain his amusement.

"I'm not sure what is so hilarious." I try to sound indignant as I challenge Daniel's act of contempt toward my concerns for sobriety.

He finally finds his breath and stands upright. He looks at me as if I am a delicate petal about to fall from its precious rose. He places one palm on each side of my face, kissing my lips gently.

"It's you, my dear. You are so very special." His lips touch mine once more, this time lingering for just a second longer. "We are artists, my dear. We can't be concerned with society's rules for us. We simply don't conform, and why should we? We must take every moment, every passion, every ounce of beauty, and live it. For then we create with that moment in time, something extraordinary to share with the world."

It is my turn to laugh at Daniel. He is able to find an excuse for whatever hedonistic acts he feels inclined to partake in. He challenges my very view of the world and I love him for it.

"Espresso martinis it is, then."

I give in to his persuasive charm once more, and Daniel sets to work on his signature cocktail. I take the time to use the bathroom to freshen up a little, splashing cold water on my face as I look into the mirror to see before me a barely recognisable version of myself. The lack of sleep and stress is taking a toll on my body, and I need to start to think of my next move very soon.

"Darling!" I hear Daniel holler from the lounge room.

This is my call to join him on the deck of the luxurious house. The sun is shining, and we look out onto the stunning white beach before us. This is a rare occasion for us to not be face down in a computer, plotting storylines or scribbling notes on character development. This morning, as Daniel instructs, we sit and take in the beauty before us. The first cocktail is inhaled in moments. The delicious blend of espresso, vodka and coffee liquor deceives the brain into believing it is an iced coffee with its smooth creamy essence.

"Another!" Daniel is on his feet, both glasses in hand before I have a chance to protest. But arguing with Daniel, I have quickly learnt, will generally be as successful as stopping a cyclone in its path. I let the buzz of the heavily laced beverage stimulate every inch of my body as the blazing sun of the late morning adds its bite to my already sensitive skin. I close my eyes and let the peaceful sounds of the crashing waves calm my mind. I could easily drift into a comfortable sleep knowing I am safe here in this fortress with my trusted friend.

"Danny?" I call back into the house to my drinking companion.

"Yes, my sweetness?" He immediately responds back in return.

"Do you think I am going crazy?" I pitch the question half in jest, hoping for an answer in the negative.

Daniel is slow to respond. I look back to see him, head bowed, formulating with care the next words that will flow from his mouth. He begins to walk toward me, drinks in both hands. He still hasn't spoken a word of reply to my plea for reassurance.

"This feels ominous." I force a small smile as I look to him for some sign of a response. Daniel takes his seat next to me and hands me the cocktail as he does. He raises his glass to mine to gently click together the delicate crystal as he considers his words.

"Here's to insanity, my dear. A most highly underrated affair of the mind."

I stop my glass short of my mouth. My reaction is raw and unfiltered. "How could you Daniel? Do you not believe anything I have told you? You think I am crazy? Imagining all of this?"

He doesn't allow the rant to continue. "Don't have a conniption, my dear!" He pauses, once he understands he has my undivided attention. "I'm just saying it all seems a little far fetched. What with a madman coming into your house, writing on mirrors, threatening your life. But yet, no one has seen him. There is no evidence that anyone was even there." He stops short of what he really wants to say. I can see him hesitate at outright calling me crazy, but his words suggest he has at least entertained the thought.

"Darling, I'm just saying. Maybe the book you are writing has inspired some fury of fantasy that has spilled over into your real life. I mean, things like that can happen for us creative types from time to time. I fall in love with my leading men all the time. I sometimes get the writing so confused in my head that I start calling my men by my protagonist's name."

"I hardly think this is the same thing," I protest for the sake of defending my honour.

"Hush, hush, my dear. We shall have no more of this debate today. I tire easily when I am bored and this conversation is clearly not doing anything to stimulate my poor brain. Drink up! Another few of these, and we are going skinny dipping out there." He informs me as he points to the sensual blue ocean in front of us.

I finally take a sip of the pleasant tasting liquid. I'm not sure how to feel about the brutally honest response to my mental health concerns. I had thought that Daniel believed me when I had shared my history of living in fear. I felt his actions to protect me were comforting. To discover he was merely placating what he thinks are my delusions of persecution make me feel somewhat foolish. But I can't disagree with his assessment of me, for those same thoughts have gone through my mind throughout the years. I dare not share the notion with anyone out loud, but I have sometimes wondered if this is all just some cruel joke of my mind.

Waiting for a madman to appear has become my life. Possibly without even recognising it, I have lived my life around someone else's agenda - allowing him to time my move from each secret location; packing up and travelling half way across the world each time in a desperate attempt to stay one step ahead. Each move he has caught up with me again forcing me to leave the friendships I have formed, the life I carved out in each location for myself in a discarded heap as I flee leaving behind no notes and no forwarding address. I dare not provide any trace that might tip the predator off to my next location.

And again, now having just felt settled for the first time in a long time, I am forced to once more contemplate my next step. The exhaustion of running is taking its toll. But what are my alternatives - to stay and fight?

"You appear deep in thought, my dear," Daniel interjects my rumination. "I can tell, because you tilt your head to the side like a cute little cocker spaniel when you are trying to work something out. It's quite endearing."

"So now I am a dog?" I play with him as I question his analogy of me to a canine.

"A cute little doggie. Maybe even a curly haired poodle." He laughs at himself as he imagines what breed of the animal I most look like.

"And you would be a Jack Russell - noisy, annoying and with lots of attitude." I add with mirth.

"Oh dear, that's vicious. You can't be mad still because I called you crazy?"

The label is a slap in the face. I want to believe it isn't true, but the reality is I worry about what I have become. My glass is empty again. The growing heat of the day provides the perfect excuse to down the chilled nectar.

"The only thing crazy about me is agreeing to sit here with you and lose another day in a haze of alcohol consumption. I'm empty by the way," I say, handing him the clear vessel for refilling.

"Oh goody! Same again, or are you ready for a new creation? A fire engine, perhaps?" he asks, on his feet and ready to take to the bar again to conjure up more magic in a glass.

"Why not? Do your worst!" The liquid drug has started to take its effect, but I dare not argue with the host. Besides being impolite, I stand zero chance of persuading Daniel to do anything other than what Daniel wants to do. Regardless of the consequences of his actions, his choices will always remain his alone.

"After this, we will partake in a nudie run and a swim I should think," Daniel says of his next grand scheme, which is clearly not open for discussion.

I think about the daring act before I respond. "What the hell? You only live once, don't you?"

And in my case, I'm not even sure how much longer I will live for.

NINE

I wake up the next morning to the sound of Daniel's mobile ringing and become acutely aware immediately of the throbbing pain in my head. Rolling over, I rub my forehead as Daniel's muffled voice answers the bleeping phone next to him.

"Yes?" His early morning after a night of drinking phone voice is much less flamboyant and decidedly more masculine than I have ever heard it before. "Who?" He questions the male voice on the other end of the line. He turns to me, his red eyes squinting through the morning sun streaming into the room. "Yes, she's here." He announces with little enthusiasm to his caller. "It's for you," he says as he hands me the mobile and rolls over onto his side, dragging with him the entire top sheet.

I am, for the first time, aware that I have once more awoken in Daniel's bed, but this time without even a vague memory as to how I got there. I scan my body for any clues, and am grateful that I am still dressed. Just in my bikini, of course, but that's better than nothing at all.

"Hello Samara?" The male voice on the mobile in my hand alerts me to his presence.

"Hello?" I answer back, somewhat hesitantly.

"Hi Samara, this is Samuel." The chipper voice loaded with enthusiasm has surely enjoyed a full and restful night's sleep. I am silent, willing my broken head to tell me who this stranger might be. I don't believe I can place the voice, nor the name for that matter.

"Samara?" the stranger speaks again. Looking for a reply or some acknowledgement.

"I'm sorry," I finally offer. "Who is this?"

"Samara, I'm Samuel. I'm a friend of Sergeant Thomas. He gave me this number to contact you, and said you were expecting my call. Have I caught you at a bad time?"

The pieces of the puzzle finally come together, and I remember the conversation from just the day earlier, the Sergeant and his kind offer of a contact specialising in self-defense training. "Yes, Samuel. I am sorry. I was asleep. It just took me a moment to work out who you were."

Samuel is the one that is silent now. "It's midday. Are you only just waking up?" he asks, accusingly. I wish I had a legitimate excuse, like say, saving lives in the emergency department all-night or recovering from jetlag, but I offer up nothing except the truth.

"Umm, I had a few cocktails last night with a friend." I stop short of saying much more.

"Oh well, I guess a night of escapism was probably what you needed considering the night I believe you had before that."

"How do you know?" I was wondering exactly how much Thomas had told his friend, including how crazy he thought I was for thinking I had a stalker trying to kill me.

"Well let's just say, Thomas was pretty keen for me to try to help. I told him I was too snowed under to take any new clients, but he was insistent that I speak to you. He seems quite the fan. He tells me you are an author."

"Yes, I guess you can say that. And you work in films, I understand?"

"Yes, I guess you can say that," he mimics me. A little chuckle is an indication that he finds the teasing humorous. "I normally do the stunt work and the martial arts scenes, but have also been given a directing spot in this latest movie. Something new to try my hand at." He adds with an obvious but unassuming pride.

"Shh, I am trying to sleep," Daniel moans at me, not moving from his position under the covers. I consider the hint and head to the door, taking the phone out onto the balcony overlooking the white sand below. Immediately the chaos of the night before comes flooding back as I view the multitude of assorted cocktail glasses, overflowing ashtrays and the remnants of a particularly illicit looking white substance, blown away perhaps by the early morning breeze.

"You have a really nice voice by the way," Samuel offers, quite off topic and out of the blue. I smile, as I find a seat at the overflowing table.

"Thanks," I reply with the tone of a giddy schoolgirl, blushing away as I accept the compliment graciously. "You do too!" I had honestly already thought it, but would normally never in a million years be brave enough to say it to a complete stranger.

"Well, thank you," Samuel says, seemingly non-perplexed by the observation. "I am actually looking forward to meeting you."

"Me too." I find myself agreeing without even needing to think about the words. I settle further into the chair, lifting my feet to perch them on the seat beside me. I rest my back against the warm fabric and smile as I try to picture what Samuel looks like.

* * *

Despite the raging headache threatening to tear my skull in two, I agree to meet with Samuel for a discussion on what it is he can offer in terms of teaching me some self-defense moves. I am aware he is incredibly busy and doing this as a favour, so I offer to drive to him on the studio lot later that day.

Security at the studios is tight. My entry is finally commissioned after the short list of guests permitted on site that day is checked and rechecked. A name badge is assigned, scanned, and ceremoniously stuck to my chest alerting all who see me that I am an approved visitor. I am given a security detail to take me to studio five, where I am told Samuel is still working with a small group of actors, who are getting a little additional direction as to how their scene is to unfold.

The room is saturated with an electric buzz. A small scene is playing out between two actors sat in the middle of the room in front of their creative leader, who is hunched forward taking in every word with genuine concentration. I become aware that I have no idea what Samuel looks like, and survey the room for a hint of recognition in a stranger's face.

The scene ends quite dramatically, and the hunched over figure steps forward to demand the attention of the acting duo. The impatient security officer, obviously keen to get back to his post, interrupts the proceedings.

"Samuel!" he yells into the centre of the space.

The director then turns to face us for the very first time. In an instant, I am mesmerised. His aqua blue eyes find mine as he stares intently for just a moment, before the realisation of who I am dawns on him. Immediately, his face breaks into the most delicious smile I've ever seen and I swear I see him lick his lips ever so quickly. His lips spread to display his gleaming white grin.

His hand is outstretched and his stride long as he covers in a microsecond the short distance between him and I. My body shakes as he takes the final step connecting in that moment, his hand to mine.

"Welcome, Samara." His voice is even more delectable in person than it was over the phone. "Please come and take a seat. You can watch the final rehearsal if you like."

I try to stammer out a few words of protest. I feel like an intruder, having taken up too much of their precious time by my obvious intrusion, but Samuel has already found a chair for me and placed it next to his in the middle of the room. "We have a special guest," he announces, addressing the gathered crowd. "This is Samara Sanders, a famous novelist. She is going to watch the scene, and we might even be fortunate enough to hear her feedback." He looks toward me once more, and presents the vacant chair for me to take my place.

As soon as I am seated, he begins the scene again. "Now from the start," he instructs the duo.

The entire roomful of artists, give their undivided attention to the acting pair as they present their obviously well-rehearsed and perfectly articulated lines. And it is fortunate for just then as the scene progresses Samuel's leg touches mine and there it is… *zing*! Not just the slight warmth of an electric current - this is a roaring flame spreading intensely through my leg, the material separating us barely comforting the skin against the searing heat that races up my thigh. We are mere inches apart, our body language mimicking each other, neither sure who is following whom.

I try not to stare as he stops the scene to address the couple in front of us. I catch a quick glance at his profile. His face is absolute perfection for a flesh and blood man, but this isn't just any man. This is the great artist, the revered creative genius everyone has come to rehearse with, and I am lucky enough to be able to sit in for a short time to take in his work. He speaks with passion as he implores the room to dig down into the depths of their deepest emotions to remember a time when the actors felt intense love. He did this all from his seated position beside me.

The words, the passion, the brilliance of his mind sparks a feeling I had long left behind. Love, but a word uttered from the mouths of mere mortals. But from his lips conjures within me a rush of adrenalin, a renewed hope that I could one day again feel this intense desire for another. This love that he speaks of, it is as if he knows exactly how to describe this somewhat indescribable quandary of emotions.

His chair scrapes against the hard, concrete floor once more, moving closer to where I sit, unable and unwilling to move from my place beside him. He leans in to become one with his audience, his presence in that small movement enticing even the most hardened of souls to engage with his desire for perfection.

Each one of them spellbound by his talent, caught up in the dizzying desire to be a part of this journey that he urges them to take with him. I look upon him again, trying not to be noticed, but his words force me to turn, to truly glance upon the virtuoso who sees into others' souls. His eyes fill with yearning, a plea for his message to be heard, for this is why they flock to him, these hordes of young artists, hoping to be inspired to brilliance today by their idol.

Once more, his arm brushes against mine, and for a second, an emotion overwhelming in nature consumes my soul. As we watch the scene unfold before us, I let out a small giggle at the awkwardness of the encounter. It is a romance, a comedy of sorts, where the female protagonist is flirting uncomfortably with her love interest. He chuckles with me, the unrest between us obvious now to both.

I once more steal a glance in his direction. His profile as he sits is intent with desire to hear the words of the young artists before him. His face is still, his mind racing with ideas to increase the presence of the characters presented to him, and I trace the profile of his face with my eyes - the proud forehead; the compassionate eyes; the rounded nose a perfect fit for his stunning face; his lips, pursed ever so slightly, concentrating, braced to speak at the first opportunity. My eyes pause for a second on his mouth, and I wonder what it would be like to kiss those lips.

He moves to face me. With a small yelp of surprise at being caught, I quickly turn my stare away. Looking down into my lap, I can feel my face flush bright red now with embarrassment. I watch out of the corner of my eye as his wide toothed smile radiates his face. Before long, I allow my eyes to slowly fall to the right once more to take in his mischievous grin. He sits there staring back at me, not in the slightest shameful for being caught returning the stare. As I raise my face to his once more, his mouth widens into a huge knowing smile. His eyes light up as they lock onto mine, and I cannot help but smile as well. A secret language between us is formed, and our conversation is silent but powerful. He feels it too. He feels the *zing*.

He lifts his arm to reach for his phone beside me, his arm crossing over my body as it reaches forward. I jump in my chair, startled by the physical closeness. His hand clenches the phone from the table to my left. The heat from his body is intense in this close proximity. As his arm returns to his lap, the side of his palm touches my thigh ever so slightly.

I race my fingers to the spot where the current sparks my skin. I glance to his face to see if he has witnessed my startled movement, but he isn't looking. His stare settles on the artists before him, his wide contagious smile still etched into his perfect features. I look forward as well, trying to subtly gasp a full breath of air into my lungs.

Never have I imagined a physical presence like his. Never before have I felt the searing heat of raw lust in one small touch. The chemical reaction my body is having to this stranger is beyond description.

He stops the performance again, imploring the artists to connect with each other.

"Look into his eyes. This is the man you adore. You want him to know how you feel. You are saying it with your words. Now, say it with your entire body. Let this man feel your desire for him."

He turns to me beside him one more time, as if teasing me with his instructions to the young artists. He sees right through me, my transparency to these intense feelings for him evident in my actions. He smiles once more with me. I feel him figuratively reach through my chest, place his hands gently around my heart and offer it a tender squeeze.

He doesn't break his glare from me as then he rises from his seat to steer the scene before us. He pounds his chest; he professes love; he draws all the air from the room, and forces every woman before him to gasp for breath.

A mere twenty minutes in his presence, the entire duration of time from the moment I have entered the room to all my breath leaving my lungs and I am in love.

TEN

Reaching the car once more in the allocated visitor space of the studio carpark and I can't wait to jump into the seat. I need to feel the safety of the metal structure around me, something to protect me from the contaminated madness in the air. I can barely breathe. I am bursting to tell someone that I just fell madly, insanely and insatiably in love. There's that word again, insane, insanity, crazy, whichever form it takes, the implication of the meaning cuts deeply. I try not to find fault with myself right now. I am sure there will be plenty of time to rehash this moment after the inevitable heartbreak sets in.

If I have truly gone mad, then at least I am going to enjoy the wild ride for a while. And what an unbelievable forty-eight hours it has been. Not only have I come face to face with my stalker, the man who wants me dead. I have enjoyed another drunken and possibly drug induced night of partying at the beach house, to wake up to a surprise phone call from the man who I have fallen madly in love with after just one brief meeting.

The chemistry is undeniable. At least from my perspective anyway and I can only imagine he feels it to. He has too. He couldn't stop smiling. That has to mean something. He tried to get me to stay but I needed to escape. Too long in his presence and who knows what a girl is capable of saying or doing. I agree to meet him tomorrow at his home to go through some basic self-defense moves. If I like it, he has offered to teach me a set of skills that will build my confidence to be home alone at night. One solution does pop into my mind and I imagine what it would be like to share my rented space with Samuel.

I try not to get too far ahead of myself but it is nearly impossible. This feeling isn't about me being lonely or alone. This feeling is entirely new. This is the first time I have ever felt this way about anyone. I'm sure my stalker ex-husband wouldn't like to hear me say that out loud, I am sure of it. After all, Robert was meant to be the love of my life.

The car is starting to feel hot and I become aware I have so far failed to turn the engine on to commence the sacred air conditioning to combat the heat of summer. I turn the key and scream as a sudden tap on the window breaks through my haze. I twist to see the smile that now melts my heart and immediately find the button to lower my driver's side window. As soon as the tinted glass has found its place inside the doorframe, his two arms are folded and perched on the windowsill. He appears in no great hurry to explain his sudden appearance at my side. He is silent.

"Can I help you with something?" I smirk at the flirty connotation to my question.

"Yes." He offers up with no further explanation. "There appears to have been a security breach." He smiles, the charm oozes from every pour of his gorgeous face. "A very serious one I am led to believe."

His smile suggests he has once again managed to find the humour in the situation at my expense. "And what would that be?" I play along to hear the words he will utter next.

His eyes have captured mine, his stare intent, as is his radiant smile. He says nothing more but reaches his arm inside the car, stretches it the width of my seat to find on my chest the security sticker, placed there only a short time before by the busy guard. He slowly tears the plastic label from my shirt, not taking his eyes off mine for even a second. The adhesive makes a slight sound as it is peeled from the material beneath it.

"I think someone forgot to check out when they strolled past the security gate." He offers by way of explanation. I barely hear his words as the warmth of his strong arm so close to my chest renders me once more speechless. The task is complete and the sticker is now dangling by the corner held by his two fingers. He lifts it to his torso, straightens from the car window and places the still functioning adhesive label on his chest, straight over the place where beneath the layers of perfectly formed muscle his heart sits.

"Goodbye Samara." He smiles as he turns to his left to walk back down the concrete path to the studio entrance. I watch as he walks away, my head turned backwards out of the car window so as to enjoy an uninterrupted view. His back is straight, his head looking forward, his arms dangling effortlessly by his side.

His legs make sure and steady lengths as the distance between us slowly increases. Then suddenly without warning he turns to look at me once more. Not losing, even a step, not stopping for a second, striding ahead and obviously needing to check to see if I was staring back at him. It is as if he knew I would be. He smiles briefly, pleased that I am indeed still entranced as I get caught again ogling this incredible looking man.

* * *

Back at the beach house, Daniel is pouring wine as I retell my story of embarrassment.

"And then he just turns to see if I am still staring, and of course, I am. I mean, how could I not?" I detail the events of the day. "But Daniel, you have to see this man for yourself. He looks like a god and the way he speaks…" My words trail off as I try in vain to explain the ways his words touched everyone in the room. "You can just tell from the way he speaks about love, that he is capable of loving deeply. He asked the actors to think of a time when they felt true romantic love for another, and I swear the female lead, she had to fan herself, her face was so flushed from excitement at hearing his words. I swear, everyone in that room felt it."

"He is an actor, isn't he?" Daniel reminds me. "So, it's all fake. It's all just an impressive and well-rehearsed act. That's what they get paid those enormous salaries for my darling. Don't be so quick to fall for the pretense." The tone of his voice is alluding to an envious rivalry with my new crush.

"Is someone a little jealous?" I tease him playfully.

"No, of course not." He snaps back, a little too quickly. "It's just that I don't want you to go getting all stupid around this actor." He almost spits the word as he says it - as if some vile poison is attached to the mere mention of the profession, which I hadn't realised until now that Daniel has very little respect for. "I don't want to be having to deal with your running mascara and drunken tears over some pretend artist, just because you think it is endearing that he can say a few rehearsed lines in front of a camera."

I laugh hysterically at the catty remark, a giggle at first that then turns into a belly laugh that I know I will have a hard time containing. The excitement of the day is expelled through the rhythmical rise and fall of my laughter, and I let it take over my body and mind. It feels good to laugh at something so trivial, making a nice change from the seriousness of the last few days.

Daniel stands over me, not interested at all in joining my spontaneous combustion of laughter and snorts. He has a look of judgement that only Daniel can master – a sneer that combines both distaste and disgust, whilst at the same time holding a fascination for the specimen in question. "So, go on already. Let's see this actor who has you all ridiculously giddy."

I reach for my phone as the idea to search for Samuel online suddenly becomes very appealing. It gives me the chance, if nothing else, to see those gorgeous blue eyes again. Daniel takes a seat beside me as I search IMDB.

Samuel isn't hard to spot. His list of movie credits is long and diverse. I click to enlarge the first photo and his wavy light coloured hair and sparkling eyes catch my companion's attention. Daniel grabs the phone from my hand, and using his two slender fingers, enlarges the image on the screen before us.

"Oh, he's a bit nice. I would do him. Let's see if he has played any cowboy roles. I do like a cute boy in chaps."

I snatch the phone from Daniel's hands, surprising both him and I with the swiftness of my movement.

"Oh, don't want to share him?" he teases me playfully. "I'll make the cocktails while you swoon over your new boyfriend." He adds as he rises from the couch to make his way to what must be his favourite place in the house, the bar.

Glancing down at the image before me on my screen, I am mesmerised. Those eyes - they can reach into a person's soul. I look to the other images, each one more enticing than the next. And there it is, the obligatory shirtless photo - a necessity I imagine for someone in his profession.

I glance over my shoulder to see if Daniel might be peering. For some reason, I don't want to share too much with him just yet. Something about his comments hurt. Although I hardly know this man, I don't want to hear my friend speaking negatively about him, for a protectiveness of him has surfaced in me already. Although maybe if I was being honest with myself it is protectiveness over what might be that I think is causing me to want to keep things close to my chest from now on.

Daniel hasn't noticed the shirtless photo from where he stands behind me in the room, which is good. He is busy nattering away to himself as he stirs the brightly coloured contents of his latest invention. I go back to my online search, and flick through the photos. He certainly has a lot, many of which have him appearing in character or dressed up at a premiere or awards ceremony. Suddenly, a loud demanding voice breaks through my daydream.

"Samara!" Daniel yells at me. "So, are you going to give me your new number or are you saving that for your little boyfriend alone?"

There is a distinct edge to Daniel's voice every time he refers to my meeting with Samuel. I feel sure of my decision to keep my little crush a bit quiet for a while.

"Samara!" he repeats, this time with even more conviction.

My mind just can't focus on anything right now. I do feel like I am walking in slow motion through a dream as Daniel joins me again on the couch, landing with a thump on the soft cushion beneath him. This is an obvious attempt to elicit a response of sympathy from me for ignoring his question about my phone number.

"You are so dramatic sometimes," I remark.

This doesn't surprise me, of course. The more I have got to know Daniel, the more flamboyant and colourful he has become. Possibly as we have become more comfortable around each other, which would make sense. And it's hilarious to watch. He speaks with such flippancy about anything to do with societal norms or expectations, but then becomes jealous and possessive at the first sign of an innocent flirtation from me.

"So, I take it from your deathly silence that only pretty boys like Brokeback Mountain cowboy there will be blessed with your new mobile number?" He takes a delicate sip of the fruity beverage, his pinky finger outstretched for dramatic effect.

I can't help but laugh. "I swear if I hadn't seen it for myself, I would place bets that you were one hundred percent homosexual. You have so many of those beautifully exaggerated behaviours that are found in the gay community."

Daniel is indignant. "And you, my dear, are simply rude. I am neither gay nor straight, and I refuse to be defined in terms evoked by your small minded, white middle class conservative society."

And there it is again, Daniel playing the dramatic radical. He is the chameleon, ever changing to fit his current mood. I dare not play with his emotions a moment longer, and decide to put him out of his misery.

"Of course, you are getting my new number," I try to assure him.

"But he got it first, didn't he?" Daniel demands to know.

My face reddens. I cannot deny the fact that I made sure I purchased a new phone on the way to the studio. How else would I have been able to contact Samuel to make a time for our first self-defense training? I can't admit the truth, nor can I lie to my friend. I simply look up at him, giving my best flirty grin in the hope that he will take pity and put the conversation to rest.

He looks at me and grunts with disgust. "Women!" With a final swig of his glass, the cocktail is finished. Mine is still sitting in front of me, not even started. "Well, drink up. I can't wait all day for you."

"Actually, I can't stay today, Daniel," I admit, sheepishly to my friend. I don't want to explain why but he is in no mood to present half facts today. I add the rest by way of explanation. "I want to have an early night. I start my training with Samuel tomorrow morning."

I don't dare look up as Daniel huffs once more, standing from the seat to stomp over to the bar to replenish his drink. I hear him mumbling again, but don't try to decipher the utterings. He is just in a mood today, and there is no reason for that to affect the first really good day I've had in a long time.

ELEVEN

The butterflies in my stomach alert me to my growing nervousness in anticipation of seeing Samuel again. They need not have, as I am all too aware from my night of tossing and turning that I would be more than just a little excited about our first training session together. And for the first night in a long time, my final thought before my eyes did close was not of my stalker. Instead, I lay picturing in my head those dreamy blue eyes and gorgeous smile of the man who, just hours earlier, was able to draw all the breath from my lungs.

Samuel's house isn't how I pictured it. In stark contrast to Daniel's immaculate home, it is a little in need of a tidy up. The garden is slightly overgrown in parts, and showing signs of neglect in places where the weeds grow longer than the grass itself. As I walk up the steep driveway, I realise that I know nothing about this man. I have not a single clue as to whether I will be greeted at the door by his wife, boyfriend, child or housekeeper. I don't even know if he has a partner, a pet, or a whole family living with him for that matter.

I feel foolish for a second to even imagine a man like him to be single and available. My whole night was spent tossing and turning over delusional thoughts of the beginning of an entire fantasy life with this man, who I have only met once. A quick Google search didn't show up any real traces of a wife or family – just a number of happy snaps with fellow actors and the occasional model, nothing to support or deny the existence of a current relationship in Samuel's life.

I hear the sound of a dog barking. It is a sizeable canine, judging from the depth of his tone in the repetition of his bark. I hope he is locked up, and I am not about to be pounded on by a vicious killer because I have dared to walk onto his private property.

I get to the top of the driveway a little out of breath. The long nights of food and alcohol working with Daniel on our book have definitely taken their toll on my body. I can feel it around the top of my legs, my stomach and arms. I have lost some muscle due to a very real lack of physical activity of late. I am proud of myself for getting back into it today, but also a little worried that I might not be fit enough at the moment to do everything Samuel instructs me to do.

I find the front entrance, a large double door made of glass and wood bearing the yin and yang symbol. Custom made, I would think. I have never seen anything like it. I take a moment to consider it further. The symbol showing up again reminds me that I have not yet got around to asking Daniel about his tattoo and how he came up with the design that bears more than just a passing resemblance to the one I sketched for myself years earlier.

This symbol itself represents the balance of good and bad, of black and white in every entity and of the importance of equilibrium in one's life. I wonder what made Samuel choose this very symbol for his front door. It seems both coincidental but also not surprising at the same time that both of my new friends in this coastal town have embraced the same symbol. I wonder if the meaning is the same for both? I smile at the simple connections to meaning that we make in our lifetime.

As my ponderings take over I reach my hand out to trace the elegant curve of the spiritual symbol carved with great care into the wooden frame that holds it.

"Samara." I tear my hand away as the door is quickly opened. Samuel is standing in front of me, smiling. He has one hand on the door handle holding it steady, the other behind his back. A huge grin greets me. And there it is all over again. That undeniable zing of chemistry as a bolt of pure adrenalin surges through my body the moment my eyes meet his once more.

"I have a present for you," he says, as he produces from behind his back a wooden stick, carved from the handle to the end with what appears to be markings of Chinese descent. "This is your Kung Fu short fighting stick. I thought you might like to start with a weapon rather than jumping straight into punching."

He wastes no time in getting to the training. I feel a little disappointed that we haven't spent some more time getting to know each other first. So many questions about him remain unanswered, but I remind myself I am after all here for the sole purpose of receiving some self-defense training. A very kind gesture of support offered by this talented man. I thank him for his thoughtfulness, and take his lead as he gestures for me to enter the house.

As I step inside, I am taken back not just by the house itself, but also by the eclectic array of offerings that adorn it. Every wall, every space in the home is filled with some detail of memorabilia. Movie posters, some from movies I had long forgotten even existed. Movies from the years before special effects and big budgets became an everyday occurrence.

We move through the house in silence, Samuel leading the way through room after room, heading with purpose for our final destination. He doesn't offer an explanation or backstory for any of the hundreds of pieces of collectables that he has obviously painstakingly sought over the years, but that doesn't stop me from taking in every inch of detail that makes up his life.

Samuel stops short of another double door entrance. He places one hand on each handle and looks back over his shoulder at me. "Ready?" He grins widely like the Cheshire cat, about to divulge the plot twist in one dramatic move.

I swallow hard. I am suddenly very nervous about the task before me rather than just the company with me. "I think so." I offer my response hesitantly.

"Don't worry, I will be gentle with you." His smile widens as my stomach does another massive flip at the ambiguous meaning behind his words.

The doors open to what I imagine is nearly a full-size martial arts studio. Unlike the rest of the house, most of the walls are white, clean and clear of decoration, except for the odd sword or fan on the walls at either end of the large room. The carpet is red in colour, and soft and spongy to walk on. Designed, I imagine with the aim of softening the blow of a hard fall to the floor.

And then I meet him - the adorable terror with the deep bark. He bounds towards me, grinning from ear to ear as he pounds the soft floor with his massive paws and wagging tail. He gains ground, and before Samuel has a chance to catch him, he leaps up onto me, knocking me straight onto my back on the ground. Fortunately, it is soft as I imagined it would be. The furry monster doesn't stop there, and jumps straight onto my chest, finding my mouth he licks my lips in a playful attack of my personal space.

"Maxwell!" Samuel's tone is serious but gentle at the same time as he grabs the dog by the collar and pulls him from me. Demanding better manners from his companion, he instructs the dog to sit while he reaches down to offer me a hand up. "I am so sorry Samara." Samuel is genuinely apologetic and surprised at the attack. "Max never jumps on anyone. He knows better than to behave like that. I am so sorry. Are you OK?"

"Don't worry about it," I reassure Samuel. "I love dogs. Is he a bulldog? How old?"

He turns to his now obedient friend beside him. "Samara, this is Maxwell. Max…for short when he is not being so naughty. He is indeed a bulldog. A normally very well behaved one-year-old boy."

"Pleased to meet you. Max." I lean down and offer a hand to shake. Max immediately understands the formal gesture, and places his large paw into my palm. I shake it gently.

"He is adorable."

"Do you have any pets?" Samuel asks.

I shake my head. "No, unfortunately not. With the amount of travel, I do, I can't have a dog."

Samuel nods his head in understanding. "I know what you mean. I miss Max so much when I am away for work. Luckily, I have a great live in caretaker who looks after him and my house when I have to go away."

This little piece of information might be the first key in the mystery of the existence, or in this case, non-existence of a partner and family. I can't help but give in to my insatiable curiosity by asking the question on the tip of my tongue. "So, you live alone then?"

"Yes." Samuel gives me the answer I had longed for. "Well, me and Max, and George, my caretaker. He is like family to me." He looks towards Max once more. "They both are, really."

Could this guy be any more perfect? He has so far proven to be gorgeous, talented, caring, passionate and loving. My heart skips a beat. I think I have met the man of my dreams.

"Would you like to make a start then?" Samuel asks.

My nervousness grows at what I might be asked to do in my first class. I feel ill prepared, having not even indulged in the slightest bit of YouTube research.

Samuel begins to speak. The lesson, it seems, has already started. "I am trained in several martial arts. What we will go through today is a combination of a few, designed to have the greatest and quickest impact in the case of a sudden attack."

I have stopped short of where he is standing. The distance between us has grown, as my body appears unwilling to walk the additional paces to where I start my instruction. He notices my hesitation, and offers up that delectable smile to me once more.

"Don't be nervous. I won't bite and we will start slowly. Do you need to warm up a little first?" he enquires.

The words in his statement could be broken down individually in so many different ways, each requiring some thought or response from me either in word or action. But I am helpless, stood still in anticipation, focusing just on the words that pertain to his mouth being on my body. *I won't bite you.* This is exactly what I heard but my writer's mind has already edited the spoken word to offer a little more detail. *I won't bite you too hard*, the romance writer in me imagines him to say.

Samuel stands, legs astride, in the middle of the room, arms outstretched as he beckons for me to join him in his place. I walk hesitantly toward him. "You look nervous."

"I am." I agree. "It's just that I haven't done anything like this before." I want to add to explain my hesitation. I hope my excuse is plausible.

He laughs at my explanation, as if it was too obvious to need to say out loud. "I should hope not. I mean, I should hope you haven't been running around hitting people with sticks too often." He laughs casually. None of this conversation appears to feel uncomfortable or awkward to him at all.

I stand in front of him now, just beyond his arm's reach. As much for his safety as for mine, I admit to myself.

"Is it OK if I touch you?" he asks gently.

My mouth is parched, and words suddenly escape me. "Why?"

He smiles reassuringly at me. "Just so I can show you how I want you to stand."

"Of course," I stammer, as if it was obvious all along and I just needed to check to make sure he knew what he was doing. I lift my hands, which up until this point, have been glued to my side. I place the tips of my fingers inside his open palms.

"OK, so this is the key to everything we will do. I want you to remember to keep your arms as your weapons. How many hands do you have for fighting?"

I believe this to be a trick question, and want to impress, but my brain has turned to pulp, and I can't even find the words for a suitably educated response. I simply shake my head, indicating I don't have an answer.

"Four." Samuel says.

He answers his own question, whilst at the same time squeezing both my hands, before reaching down to my elbows and twisting them ever so slightly to show how my elbows become weapons as well. The plan to try to keep him at arm's length, for at least a little while anyway, has failed miserably. I can feel the heat on my skin where his hands are, and almost need to pull them away before they suffer a more severe irritation, but I can't think of anything I would rather do less than to break physical contact with my gorgeous instructor.

To my surprise, I manage to last the length of the session without embarrassing myself too much. Unfortunately, Samuel keeps it strictly professional. No idle chitchats about any possible boyfriends in my life and no little bits of information about his personal life given away. The close contact with each other not dissipating in the slightest the enticing touch of his skin against mine. The hour and a half of training seems much longer in reality, with the complete concentration required to master every manoeuvre ensuring time took a different measure.

Samuel is encouraging of my initial progress, even suggesting that next session we can build on our existing skills to incorporate some kicking possibly. I am not sure how any of this will make a difference if faced with my stalker again, though I hold a slight hope that if I practice enough, instinct might kick in and my body could automatically go into fight mode.

I too am keen to see how much more he can teach me. The thought of leaving him today saddens me, and I secretly hope he offers a further training time in the very near future.

He opens his mouth to speak and the words flow out with ease. "Would you like to have dinner some time?" he requests quite out of the blue. His confident smile is replaced with what appears to be a nervous twinge.

"Like a date?" Before the words had left my mouth, I already know the damage I potentially have done to our new friendship. Me, stupid enough to assume that Samuel would want to take me on a date, speaking the words out loud that should have remained a mere doubt in my head.

"Yes, like a date." The smile returns to his face, pleased now at my response.

"But why?" I tilt my head to the side - the gesture Daniel has jokingly referred to as my thinking face that makes me look like a dog. I catch myself doing it, and look down to the floor, unsure of what gesture would seem more attractive.

"Why not?" Samuel is doing this annoying thing, where he almost parrots my failed attempt at honest communication. "How often does a beautiful, talented, creative woman like yourself walk into my life? Why wouldn't I want to take you out on a date?" He is confident. I like that about him, whereas my current mode of operation borders on the clinically insane.

"Well, it's just that I thought you would meet women everyday with the work that you do, and you know, I wasn't even sure if you were single."

"It's best not to date where you work," Samuel says, flippant in his explanation. "And single, yes. Never married. What about you?"

"Um, I was married. Separated now."

"Separated, not divorced?"

"Um, divorced. Not too sure about that."

He smirks a little, clearly unsure what to make of my response. "You are not sure if you are divorced or not?"

I didn't want to get into anything further at this stage. The answer isn't as simple to explain as one might imagine. "Long story." I offer as a meagre reply to what should be a fairly straightforward answer.

"Maybe the kind of story best shared over a bottle of wine and dinner," he suggests hopefully.

"Or maybe two…" I add. He looked slightly confused. "Two bottles of wine, that is."

He understands completely my connotation. "OK, so it's a very long story then that we share over two bottles of wine." His smile radiates once more, having worked out the details of what I assumed would be our next meeting. He leans in and kisses my cheek every so lightly. I catch myself nearly turning to meet his lips, though fortunately, my head caught my body in time to stop me.

"OK." I feel the urgent need to leave. "Until then," I reply in a non-committal tone.

"Tomorrow night?" he offers as a suggestion.

"Tomorrow night." I agree, as I nod my head in the gesture accustomed to greeting samurai.

I sincerely hope in the next twenty-four hours I can find within me the ability to utter more than just a few nonsensical words for any reply to this man. I am a writer, after all. Surely, I can find some way to articulate with more than just the written word. My verbose capabilities have failed me dramatically, so I vow to have some suitable conversation starters ready in time for our dinner.

TWELVE

The chances of sleep tonight will be slim, if at all. My mind is racing over the possibilities of what the next day may hold, and my heart feels full and light, the way I imagine it should feel if the burden of my stalker and pending death didn't occupy every minute of my life. I feel hopeful for the first time in a very long time. The fact that I was beginning my planning for my next move, my necessity for staying one step ahead of death was just a mere detail that I decided to avoid. At least for the time being so I could focus on having some fun for once.

Enjoying a date, a bottle of wine, a first kiss, perhaps, with a gorgeous man is a daydream that I will indulge, even if it is for just a day. I figure I deserve the delightful distraction. Ever since leaving my husband, my life has become one long unknown. I have no idea where I will spend Christmas, my birthday, or any other special occasion for that matter. Worrying too far in advance about anything has become a luxury I know I cannot indulge in.

So, at peace I feel, I decide to run a warm bath. I search the house for scented candles and the facemask I have been eager to try, and gather together my laptop and Bluetooth speaker for a little musical serenading while I relax in the scented bubbles. The thought of my laptop, my precious holder of creative records, falling into the bath is of some concern, so I ensure I bolster it on the bathroom bench with some additional support. I would have normally used my phone for such a cause, but have so far failed to download the necessary apps and music that my last phone had stored so reliably for me.

As I step one foot inside the hard surface of the tub, I sigh at the slight sting of the warm water on my skin. I step my other foot through the froth of the bubbles, and let my body fall into the warm embrace of the miracle liquid known as water. Water soothes my soul, whether it is the ocean, my tears, the rain, or a bubble bath. Water brings with it a healing power that I cannot explain. I can never be far from the water for long. Of all the places I have called home, most were but a short drive from a lake, the beach, or even a city-strewn river.

I don't want to think about any of that right now. I want to give my brain permission to switch off for just a moment - a day, even. I want to pretend, for a brief time, that my life is normal. I want to pretend that I am merely a woman thinking about her first date with a man, imagining the possibilities, nervous by the newness of it all. I yearn for the life that I can no longer have. I crave the life that has been ripped apart by the bloody desire of a madman to end it.

But this is the key question here. Why hasn't he already? Why didn't he kill me the other night in this very house? Why didn't he take my life? He could have easily done it. As he himself imagines, I have grown to believe that he will get away with it. I know how he lives his life with meticulous detail. He has had enough time and planning to carry out the perfect murder, and end the days of his life in peace, living to a ripe old age.

For some reason, he will get the life that I will not. He will get to love again, possibly marry. Possibly raise children, if he hasn't already. It is surprising at how little I now know about the man I once shared my bed with. He was a someone to me at one point. At first he was a stranger, then he became my lover, before becoming a stranger once more. And for what purpose? The entire time we were together, he did nothing but to chip away at the person I once was. My writing became the topic of jokes. Not earning enough money from my novels to appease him, my writing was considered just a wasteful hobby. My looks, deteriorated with the stress becoming something to be critical of and my body not being cared for became a thing of ridicule to my husband.

All of his bitterness and hatred, one day following another eroded everything that I was. My family lost; my friendships untenable following so many rejections to social invitations; my small savings no longer my sole responsibility, but at the whims of a controlling husband to decipher. And it all happened in the blink of an eye. One moment, a gentleman was asking me on a date; the next, I was huddled in a ball on the floor, wishing and praying for it to open up and bury me beneath the solid earth.

A creak of the wooden floorboards on my back deck drags me from my painful memories to the reality of the here and now. I no longer jump at such noises in the dark. They scare me no more, for I know, without a shadow of a doubt, that my end will come at a time of his choosing. I will have no warning, no recourse, but to do whatever I can with what opportunity presents.

I think back to the day's training with Samuel. It was empowering – exhilarating, really - to imagine that I could conjure up enough power and strength from my body to defend myself in an attack.

I am curious as to how much more there is for me to learn, and wonder how much longer I will be able to stay around to enjoy his lessons. In an attempt to rid myself of unpleasant thoughts once more I picture Samuel's blue eyes staring into mine as his gentle hands, with grace and precision, went about contorting my limbs to perfect each strike. My body rotating at the hips to produce power that ran through my arms into the stick to meet with deadly force the padded mitt in his hand.

I mentally rehearse the movements, smiling as I think of the time spent today with Samuel. I must remember to thank Sergeant Thomas for his kind introduction, perhaps with another signed book for his wife? That would be the least I could do. My mind suddenly fills with the tasks needing to be checked off between now and my date tomorrow night - nails, hair, something to wear. I close my eyes, and try to visualise my to-do list as my body drifts into a peaceful state of relaxation. I feel my body begin to fall into a slumber, and I do not fight it.

* * *

As I jolt upright, I unintentionally splash the now tepid water onto my face as I startle. I awake with the remnants of something unusual around me. The noise I heard, was it in a dream or in the house? I sit still and silent. I need to hear it again before I can decide. I feel my heart pound in my chest, suddenly aware of my nakedness in the bathtub. I am laid open and most vulnerable without my clothing. I don't dare move from what feels to be my safe haven for the moment. My breathing is deep and measured, in and out, as the air rapidly fills my lungs just as they try to expel it. I attempt to concentrate for a moment on my breathing, hoping to avoid another panic attack. Not now, not like this.

Do I detect faint footsteps or is it my imagination running away from me? It is becoming more difficult to distinguish reality from fiction the longer this nightmare continues. I am genuinely fearful. I thought I was past feeling scared by the bumps in the dark of the night. They are the things I fear the most. The unknown. The doubt I have of myself. Not trusting my instincts to know what is real, and therefore, not trusting my mind or body to react in time to prevent my certain death.

The noise, it could be a possum or cat on the deck, their small claws scratching the timber as their delicate body glides softly across the boards in search of food or an opening to the house. I instantly do a mental check. Did I lock the sliding door that leads to the deck? I can't be sure in this moment of uncertainty. But it is too late anyway for just in that second of doubt, the noise becomes clear. It is a door shutting. The sliding door is closed shut. I close my eyes for I know the end is near.

He is here again. Robert is inside the house once more.

I do not hesitate now as I step from the bath, and reach for my robe to throw on my naked, now trembling, body. The little comfort the sheer fabric provides will offer nothing in the form of protection once he decides he will harm me. I stop for a second, wondering whether I should blow out the candles that set the atmosphere for my little piece of heaven. I wonder if the darkness that ensues once the candles are distinguished will provide some additional benefit to my cause. I turn, and with a force of breath, blow out the last of the light to fill the house. There is total darkness before me, and in doing so, before him as well.

He will surely know where I am now from the sudden disappearance of the light of the flickering candles, and the cascading of the water as I reef my body from the tub. He will have undoubtedly noticed and will be poised ready to attack as soon as I leave the safety of the bathroom. I raise my face to the ceiling, letting my head drop back for just a second as I inhale a deep breath into my lungs, possibly my last. I draw on every last strength I have to take that first painful step into the unknown darkness.

And just as I do, the sliding door opens and closes again. I hear the footsteps bound not delicately this time, but with great force as they hurdle their mass to the stairs to make their hasty retreat. For some strange reason, I follow the footsteps to the deck, sliding open the huge glass door as if it is the weight of a feather. I bound across the deck in the hope of a glimpse of my retreating stalker. Something feels strange. His presence is different. It doesn't feel like Robert striding across the deck. I see nothing of the man I assume is my ex. I do not detect the scent of his skin in the air. I don't think it was him.

A sudden thought occurs to me. What if the intruder was indeed a stranger? Not my stalker, but a random offender looking for a quick pile of cash or jewellery to pawn. I run back into the house, careful this time not to close the door to in any way dilute the vital evidence of fingerprints the police may need to prosecute in case of a burglary. My brain has finally kicked in and is telling my body to check the bedroom for sign of theft.

I run into my darkened room. The fear that overcame me moments earlier is replaced with a curiosity to find answers to the identity of the stranger in my house. I switch on the bedroom light. The room is unscathed, unharmed in any way. My brand-new phone sits on my bedside table on charge just as I had left it. My jewellery, or what little I have left, is stored neatly inside its casing. For some unknown reason, I check my wardrobe to find that my clothes, the few that I keep to travel from place to place, are neatly sitting on their hangers.

I step into the kitchen, although there is little to be stolen here. I walk into the lounge room to find the furniture all in its rightful place. The large television screen, barely used, is still firmly attached to the wall. I walk through the house no need for further lighting as my eyes become well-adjusted to the dimly lit dwelling. I prefer the dark of night to artificial lighting as a rule. So, in tune with the outdoors, spending as much of my time at the beach as I can at the moment, I relish the cool dim surrounds of nightfall when I am home.

I am no longer scared of the dark, for within it holds nothing that isn't also present in the light. Human being's manufactured fear of the night is merely a societal suggested norm perpetuated by screenwriters and directors across the globe. Storylines suggest anything that is fearful and deadly will happen to you at night or in your sleep. I only wish this was the case for me. For in daylight, at night, in the earliest most beautiful moments of sunrise or sunset, I still feel fear. I feel it. I taste it. I know it with every sense of my being. There is no longer reason to assume that my death will happen in this house, at night, when I am alone. Who knows when or how it will happen, except to know that eventually it will happen.

Reassured that I am indeed alone in the house, I remember the bath, the music softly serenading me and I return to the bathroom to clear my indulgent mess of bubbles from the tub. The hard tiles are slightly damp from the water that dripped from my skin as I stalled to leave the sanctuary of the bathroom. In the darkness, my feet find the bathroom mat, and connect with it. The soft, fluffy piece of material that secures wet feet to the floor is slightly damp. I stand on something solid on the mat. I stall, frozen for a second for my brain to analyse the hard, cylindrical shape lying dormant on the floor.

I let the sole of my foot discover the item for a second longer, hoping that my mind will catch up and recall the discarded object which clearly has no place being on the bathroom floor. A warm sticky substance covering the object leaves patches of debris on my foot. I am confused as to what I could have left here. The object feels vaguely familiar, but not in its current location. I turn and switch the light on, and see with my eyes the object left as a message for me. My Kung Fu fighting stick, which prior to my bath had found a home atop my bedroom chest of drawers. Left there, as a constant reminder that I need to practice. A little piece of comfort, that I was finally taking some strategic steps toward my own personal safety.

But here the stick lies not in my room where I had left it but on the bathroom floor. The room I had left only moments earlier to search the house for signs of the intruder. I bend down to pick the stick up. Uncertain about everything including the misplaced sense of safety I had felt moments earlier when I believed a mere burglar had entered my house by sheer coincidence. I bring the stick closer to me. The sticky substance that found its way to my foot is now all over both hands. The thick red covering has a smell that is undeniable in nature. It is blood.

I close my eyes and pray that the blood on the stick is not human.

THIRTEEN

I scream as I drop the stick back down on the bathroom floor and feel a flood of tears begin to explode from my eyes. I run for my phone, praying it is still there. I recall the last number dialed from my contact list, the last phone call I made to ensure I had the details of the meeting with Samuel correct. It rings.

I scream into the phone begging him to pick up. "Answer! Please answer!"

The ringing lasts forever. With each unanswered second, the chances of the scenario I fear the most becomes more likely. I close my eyes, and say a silent prayer. The phone disconnects. The call is left unanswered.

I drop to the floor, the tears now freely flowing. I scream out into the darkness. I know that my stalker, my ex-husband is not far away. Inside my house, he has become comfortable, not afraid to hide in the shadows as I move from room to room. He is so close, and yet appears to bear me no harm. The torture is in the waiting.

My tears do not mask the picture forming in my head. The image of my new friend laying in a pool of blood somewhere floods my brain. This imagined end to his life, being his punishment for doing nothing more than to help me. Samuel is so strong, he would have fought back - the one person I would imagine could defend himself from the carefully constructed attack perpetrated by my stalker. I cannot believe I did this to him.

The phone sounds. I look down and see his name.

"Samuel!" I scream into the phone, his name muffled between my sobs. "Are you OK?"

"Samara, I'm sorry I missed your call. What's wrong?"

"I am so glad to hear your voice. I was worried something had happened to you."

"I'm fine. What's going on? You sound panicked? Did something else happen? Do you want me to come over?"

I finally take a deep breath. I have been holding it in, the precursor for a certain panic attack. "No, I am fine," I finally concede. "I am sorry if I woke you. I just got a fright. I'll explain all tomorrow."

"I am happy to come over if you want. You don't sound well."

"No, please don't worry. I am fine. It is nothing really, and I will explain all. Good night. Get some sleep. I will see you tomorrow."

I end the call. The relief is overwhelming, but I know there is little chance of me sleeping at all tonight. I make one more call. The recipient picks up immediately. My caring friend, Daniel always at the ready to take a call from me, as if he has become accustomed to the unexpected twists and turns that are my life.

"Daniel, can you come over please? I don't want to be alone."

He doesn't ask for further explanation. "On my way, my darling."

* * *

I collapse onto the floor beneath me, suddenly aware of the enormity of the situation. If that isn't Samuel's blood on the stick, then who or what does it belong to? I am vaguely aware of the noises under the house. I haven't closed the sliding door to the deck, but what value security-wise at least has it proven to be up to this point? I don't doubt that my stalker is nearby. He always is. I can feel him. But that's the strange difference tonight. That person who ran from my deck, although I didn't see him through the darkness, it didn't feel like it was my ex-husband.

I know Robert's body language well. His mere presence conjures up a sick feeling in my stomach. The same feeling that often leads to my panic attacks. When he is around I feel nauseous. My head hurts; my heart pounds and I feel hot. I know it well, for this was the way I felt for the long years of marriage to him. It was a constant feeling of unrest, just waiting for the next eruption. Just waiting to be yelled at, abuse and names hurled at me like I was there for the soul purpose of emotional release for the abuser.

The abuse went on for more than a decade. It was years upon years of the not knowing what to expect; of not knowing when the next outburst was going to happen. This was the feeling I got every time I was in Robert's presence. This feeling of unrest, of the unknown, of being totally within another's control. But tonight, it felt different. Innocent almost, like game playing. Tonight, felt almost as if someone was playing a childish prank. Unfortunately, this childish prank involved real blood, not imagined.

"Hello, my dear is anyone home?"

"Daniel, I am in my bedroom," I yell out into the darkness.

"Oh, this is all very dramatic isn't..." He stops short as he sees me for the first time. "Oh, darling. What have you done? Are you hurt?" The blood on my hands is evident. My tear filled reddened eyes a sure sign that something horrible has happened. I must have blood smeared everywhere – the blood from the stick, the unknown victim's blood drying on my hands and everywhere else that I have come into contact with. The phone, the carpeted floor beneath me, my hair and my eyes are all covered in the thick red substance.

"He was here again."

"Who?" Daniel asks, wide-eyed.

"My ex-husband, of course. Who else?"

We sit in silence. Me huddled on the floor next to my bed. My phone firmly grasped in my hands. I take a moment to remember what it is I need Daniel for. "Let me show you."

I jump from the floor, my enthusiasm to share my nightmare with another soul coming not from any deranged satanic virtue but from the perspective of a problem shared. I step inside the bathroom. The light is still on, the bath still full. The bubbles now dissolved with time. The music still plays, ever so slightly. A song I remember from long ago, a song about heartbreak.

Daniel is a step behind me now. Gaining in enthusiasm upon seeing the bloodied mess I have become. Growing in concern, or at least I hope for my plight. Enthused to find out what has happened and where all the blood has come from.

I walk over to the bathroom mat and pick up the fighting stick. It is blunt on each end, not meant to pierce the skin, but instead to inflict a strike so forceful it renders the assailant useless long enough for my escape. I raise the wooden weapon to Daniel's face. "This is what I trained with today with Samuel. I found it here on the floor covered in blood."

Daniel looks first to the stick and then to the bathroom floor, itself covered with blood, fortunately concentrated mainly on the bath mat but seeping ever so slightly into the white tiles beneath it.

Daniel looks at it with quiet consideration. "What happened? How did it get here? Whose blood is that? Did you do this?"

"No!" I scream back at him. "He was here. I heard him enter the house, and I went to confront him, and then I checked my bedroom, and couldn't find him, and then I came back into the bathroom and it was here." I know I am not making sense as I try to explain everything at once.

"Did you see him? The guy that was here?" Daniel asks tentatively.

"No, but I am not entirely sure it was him. It felt different. His presence didn't feel as threatening."

"Well, we have nothing to be concerned about then, do we?" And with that flippant remark, Daniel grabs the stick from my hand and throws it into the bathtub. The blood from the stick immediately begins to blend with the soapy water.

"Daniel!" I yell at him. "That is evidence for the police."

"Police? What have they ever done for you? Or me, for that matter." And with the flick of a wrist, he picks up the bloodied bath mat and throws it into the bath water as well.

* * *

It is hours later, and Daniel has sourced every last ounce of alcohol in the house to blend something drinkable, in his own words, to calm me down. Initially, I am furious that Daniel has potentially destroyed the first real piece of evidence of the intruder that I have been able to collect during the years that my stalker has tormented me, but in the end, I agree with his argument. The police have done nothing to offer me even the slightest form of encouragement to help me keep myself safe.

Daniel reminds me that the fighting stick is mine, so my prints are potentially all over it. As are Samuel's fingerprints, come to think of it. I can't rely on the competence of our current police force to ensure that they don't mix up prints and suddenly accuse Samuel of a murder he didn't commit. I did feel bad that potentially an innocent victim has somehow suffered in all of this, but I keep telling myself the blood could just as easily have come from fresh road kill, or an especially bloody offcut from the local butcher.

I don't feel in my heart that I know the answer to any of this, but I also don't have the energy to spend vast amounts of time hypothesising about the source of the blood either. What I do know about husbands that kill their partners is they are not normally a major threat to anyone but their partner. There is something quite particular about their murderous intent.

I feel tired, or drunk or both. The sun is rising. I can see it from the deck. I don't know if I have dozed a bit in between theorising with Daniel, or if we have managed to keep each other suitably entertained for the entire night. I don't guess it matters. We are both still here and still breathing. Samuel is OK. My stalker is nowhere that I can see or feel his presence for now and I have survived yet another night.

How many more nights I have left I cannot know, but last night, I did something that I have never had the strength to do before. I felt determined to face my attacker - not just simply sit and wait for the onslaught, but to present myself to him face to face, and potentially disarm, or at the very least, defend myself. I guess there is something to this self-defense idea after all.

I look down to see a smear of blood on the side of my hand. This stuff sticks to everything. Luckily, I guess, for the souls that depend on it to pump oxygen through the body. I can't help but wonder where the blood came from. I fear that question may haunt me for as long as I live. If it is up to a certain someone, that won't be that long anyway.

"Samara!" Daniel almost shouts from the couch in the corner of my deck. "I'm sleepy. Drag me to a soft mattress." I sometimes wonder who is looking out for whom in this friendship. Daniel, although appearing at the speed of light when I needed him, did little throughout the night to validate my concerns about the source of the evidence of an intruder.

He does make quite a statement about police indifference in this small coastal town, and for that, I am grateful. To think without his influence, this rented house could have today been the scene for forensics, investigators and media alike. Not to mention the celebrity hype, as he likes to call it, when they find out a published author is the owner of the said "murder weapon."

I don't want to push my luck in trying to drag Daniel to the nearest guest room, so instead grab a plush throw and tuck him in on all sides. He appears to melt into the warm comfort it provides, and closes his eyes tightly to enjoy some slumber. I stand for a moment, watching the peace with which he sleeps. A peace I have not known for many years. I decide to join him, carefully unraveling one side of the warm blanket to make a small creep hole. I venture in, and create for myself the position of little spoon as I wrap his sleeping arms around my middle and close my eyes. One way or another, sleep will come to me.

Murderous Intent

FOURTEEN

I am barely functioning today - hardly energetic enough for a date, let alone the amount of work I will need to do to get the house back in order. My home is a disgusting mess, thanks to the new stains of the carpets that need soaking. Another night of Daniel-induced cocktails didn't help with the clean-up process. Strangely, he seems to be impeccably clean in his own home, but a raging mess in mine. I can't complain though, because according to him, I dragged him from the best episode yet of his favourite reality show. I have never known Daniel to watch television, but I guess everyone has his or her own little guilty pleasures.

Daniel was up surprising early, and keen to get home. I suspect he had a bit of a rendezvous himself too, but was keeping very secretive about it all. His phone didn't stop alerting him to messages during his time at my house, so I am guessing it might be something fresh and new. I make a mental note to quiz him some more about it next time I see him. We can swap dating stories, hopefully both having positive news to report. I smile as I imagine Daniel and I double dating. I picture a civilized dinner, just Samuel and I, Daniel and his partner. What woman wouldn't enjoy a date with three gorgeous men?

I spend the day cleaning my house, completing washing, and doing a little bit of shopping at the local organic market - anything I can do to keep the nerves at bay as I try not to think ahead to staring into those mesmerising blue eyes of Samuel's over dinner. I try to remember back to a wise quote I once read, but I fail to remember the words exactly. Something along the lines of how a life can change in a mere twenty-four hours. A life can be lost, a new one created, a love found, a child born. One day, one simple rotation of the sun, and a person's life can be changed forever.

As I reflect, I begin to feel a bit more like that myself. Yesterday, I was taking my first lesson with Samuel. Last night, I was left fearing my life was at its end, and today, I am hopeful again. Hopeful of this new connection with Samuel - a special someone who seems to want to enter my life, a soul mate of sorts. Maybe it's too early to be using such a strong sentiment, but I am feeling more excited by the minute to spend time tonight with someone who, for one reason or another was meant to be in my world. I smile to myself again as my body tingles all over at the thought of the endless possibilities with this talented and passionate man.

The day drags on as it does when there is something to look forward to, but finally I am ready. Showered, dressed, moisturised, contoured, perfumed, and enjoying the butterflies in my stomach as I begin to head for the door. I search my house for my car keys, again lost in the chaos that is quickly becoming my life. Samuel, the caring soul that he is, did offer to drive, which I appreciate but I think it best if there is a distinct beginning and end to this date.

I feel it is best tonight to try to avoid that awkward moment when you wonder whether you are supposed to ask your date if they want to come in for a drink as you fumble around to find your door key in your bag. The intensity of the chemistry I feel for Samuel leaves me in no doubt that I would definitely be asking him to come in if he was to drive me home.

I lock the house, taking special care to leave at least two lights on to establish the pretense that someone is home. I double-check that the lock on the front door is in its secured position just before I pull it closed. My car has been left outside for convenience from when I returned earlier in the day from my quick dash down the road to the shop. The shiny silver vehicle is gleaming in its position on the drive after having enjoyed a full detail earlier in the day. A thorough wash and polish giving the car a little extra sparkle and hopefully ridding it of any final traces of sand from my special message left for me on the front seat.

My nervous energy has me both smiling and shaking at the same time. I am looking forward to spending these hours with Samuel and am in awe of this talented man. I imagine sitting across the table from him and wonder if I will again feel that moment of zing - that electric current that is undeniable every time his skin touches mine.

The car starts up, and of course, is filled with sexual innuendo from the lyrics of the hit of the week. It is a curious phenomenon. When you don't have sex for so long, you can almost forget it even exists. Then, when you meet someone, it seems to be all you can think about. That exciting first phase of a new relationship when you can't get enough of each other can be quite addictive.

The roads are clear, as they often are in this sleepy little town. I'm thankful to have known such a place in my lifetime, for these small pieces of paradise will one day be replaced by high-rise tourist havens. It will all happen so very quickly too, I imagine. One day the houses like the one Daniel owns will be turned into apartment blocks or commercial ventures, the land too expensive for just a residential dwelling for one. For now, the peace and quiet of the road ahead is just what I need to focus on. I daydream about the next few hours of exquisite company I am about to enjoy.

The sudden distinct noise in the back right tyre sounds more like a release of gas than it does a blow-out. It is quiet and non-foreboding, but still loud enough to be heard over the music. It is an instant later - not even seconds, but less - that the tyre is destroyed. My ability to steer the car is now defunct. I look around, and am grateful that I am alone on the road as I ease on the brakes, and begin to attempt to manoeuvre the vehicle as best I can off the road. I remain calm, for I know it is the only way to survive this situation. I am experienced, unfortunately, this isn't the first time my tyre has been damaged.

The car wobbles limply to its resting place on the side of the road. The scraping of the metal rim against the asphalt on the hard road is surely doing untold damage to the wheel itself. I let out a deep breath as I manage to bring the car to a halt. It's not an ideal location to stop, so I immediately engage the hazard lights, search for my phone and as I locate it, I move across the front seat to climb out onto the shoulder of the road. I walk the few paces down the street to jump the safety barrier, and find myself knee deep in long grass. My bare feet find the cool ground beneath them stimulating.

I bend over to breathe, but before I am aware of it coming, my stomach has emptied the contents of my lunch onto the green blades of weeds in front of me. I wipe the remnants of the act from my mouth, my red lipstick, applied with care only moments earlier is smeared onto the back of my palm. I turn my hand over to look to my phone for rescue. The screen is black, and I press the button to engage it into action.

The panic I have been suppressing begins to rise, as I fear my battery hasn't charged properly. Suddenly, the screen comes alive and the light illuminates my face. I allow a slight sigh to pass through my lips, grateful that I will soon have some assistance. My stomach unclenches as the relief fills my body. I begin to scroll through to try to locate the number of the roadside service, part of the package provided on my leased vehicle. I attempt to search for details, but the contacts list is bare. No numbers exist on the phone.

I fear I know what has happened, and I look at the small icon on the top left of the screen to indicate the presence of an active sim card. There is none. The phone is charged, but without the presence of that small micro sim, it is rendered absolutely useless. Before I have time to process my next move, the headlights of an approaching vehicle catch my attention. This is the first passer-by since my car faulted and I sought refuge in the scrub alongside the road. This is, of course, my fault for choosing to take the quiet back road from my house through to the commercial area.

I quickly step over the rail to wave the car down. Frantically, I move my arms now so as to not miss this chance for assistance. The driver catches me in the headlights and quickly slows to pull the car onto the shoulder in front of mine. I stand patiently, waiting for them to alight the vehicle to thank them for their help. In the dark street, void of any over-the-road lighting, I struggle to see how many passengers the modern looking sedan is carrying. It feels an eternity, waiting for the driver to step out of the vehicle, so I decide to walk toward them. I take to the side of the road, furthest away from potential traffic. I'm being overly careful really, as the chance of a speeding vehicle plowing me down is highly unlikely on this quiet street.

As I near the stranger's car, my bare feet tread carefully on the loose gravel and slithers of glass on this section of the road. I see the driver's side door open, and with that, the interior lights of the sedan light up. There is only one person in the car – a man, I presume, from the cut of his hair. He is tall, his head coming incredibly close to the ceiling above him. His shoulders are square and strong. He isn't an overly large man but holds himself with a real presence.

His gloved hand holds the door open as he alights the vehicle. I don't need to see the face. I know exactly who has come to my rescue. I turn around to look through the dark night in the hope for another vehicle. The road either side is clear of human life. There are no houses in this immediate area - just long stretches of undeveloped land for as far as I can see with the current lack of illumination. My hands involuntarily clench into tight fists, and I feel my stomach begin to cramp as I turn my head in every direction - unsure whether I should run and hide, or stand and fight.

My ex-husband steps out of the vehicle. He immediately turns to me, an arrogant smile plastered from ear to ear across his face.

I am frozen. The automatic response communicated from my brain to my body is to freeze in place. The age-old question of what my immediate response to danger is answered once more, as I can't find the ability to move a limb. Every person has the response of fight, flight or freeze, when given a deadly stimulus, and unfortunately for me, the flight and fight are neither strong nor automatic enough to allow me to defend or rescue myself. Instead, my brain, my muscles and my mind all align to hold me in position. Defenseless, awaiting my demise as if the end was designed to always happen this way.

"Hello my darling wife." The words drip from Robert's mouth like the vile poison they are.

I want to run. My head is dizzy with panic. My feet betray me, as they stay plastered to the bitumen beneath them. I am unable to answer. I close my eyes for the briefest of seconds in the hope that when I reopen them, he has disappeared - just a ghost in the night, a figment of my vivid imagination. My eyelids spring open but he is still here in front of me, closer than ever, having traversed the short distance between us with a calm, slow swagger.

"Stop!" I manage to yell as I raise my palm to detain him in his place.

The distance between us is minimal now, as the length of my arm fills the narrowing gap and his smile widens as he enjoys the sight of terror on my face. This emotion, he evokes in me with ease. His stride determined. He will reach me in a split second. My chest tightens at what is to come as he raises his arms outstretched, welcoming me into an embrace. My skin reacts the moment his hands touch it. He is close now, every inch of his body pressing against mine as his arms tighten around me and squeeze. The warmth of his breath against my neck sends a shiver down the length of my spine.

I say nothing. Nor does he. I am still. My arms are against my side, pinned to my body under the weight of his embrace. I feel his head turn, his mouth now against my skin. He purses his lips and kisses my neck, inhaling my scent like a predator sensing the weakened resolve in their victim's blood. He is so close, and I have no form of protection available to me, except to not fight him.

Utilising the well-practiced technique of dissociation, I attempt to leave my body, to let my mind wander to a happier place, a safer time where my life isn't at risk. I don't want to feel the pain of what is to come, my imminent doom. He turns his mouth to my ear. He allows the warmth of his exhaled air to linger over the sensitive organ.

"You smell delicious, my beautiful wife." His hushed tones provide no clue yet as to his intent. "Just as I remember." His abhorrent words exist long after the sound of his voice has dissipated.

I say nothing. There are no words to reply.

"Let me take you home," Robert whispers eagerly to me.

The sound of his voice offends every sense in my body. That word, *home* resonates with a place I long left behind, a place of sheer terror where one excruciating day followed the next. It was a house, but not a home - more a fortress where my liberty was taken from me;

a place of pure pain; of horror I wish my mind would forget. I anger at his use of the word that should hold such loving memories.

I take a step back from him, and in that instant, apply every ounce of force my body will afford me to break the physical prison created by his hold.

"Just leave me alone!" I scream out into the darkened night. Not so much at him as to the dark force field that his presence has created around me. I can feel the tears well behind my eyes. I have no resolve when he is near. The energy it takes to break his hold is all my body can muster. The delicate balance of chemistry that floods the brain now alerts my body to the danger. My fingers start to tingle. My stomach knots and my chest heaves.

The pain begins in my left side. It catches my breath, and this time, alters my vision as well. My head lops from one side to the next as the sections of my brain no longer required for higher order functioning begin to shut down. My body is alert to the threat to my life, and is responding in the only way it knows how. My most severe panic attack ever has begun. I only hope it is swift.

I fall to the ground, and crawl to the side of the road before the bile erupts from my throat, falling onto the dark hard ground at the place where the bitumen meets the earth. I cannot turn to see him, for I am lost in the pain that is searing heat through my chest. I try desperately to gasp for air into my lungs. I cannot concentrate on anything more than staying alive until this physical attack on my body passes. I repeat the words over and over in my head – *breathe, breathe* - but it does nothing more than heighten my urgency for oxygen. The pain is unbearable. My chest feels as if it will implode and I suddenly become fearful that this might not be just another ordinary panic attack.

I sense his dark force leaving. I look up to see him walk toward his car. Leaving me in this state on the side of the road, in the middle of the night. No phone coverage, a vehicle that won't drive, and no one to help me if I am in fact taking my last breaths of life. But this is typical of him. Unable to stand being around what he would call an overly emotional woman. He always hated to see me cry, not ever providing anything in the way of comfort. He lorded over me when he was angry, forcing me to bear witness to his fits of rage, but when it came time for me to dissolve into tears he walked away each and every time.

How did he not see that we were suffering the same emotional anguish? My husband during our marriage - fed up with his work; with chores; with his daily responsibilities; and with life in general - taking every last ounce of his negative emotions out on me. And me, his wife - sworn to honour, taking the abuse the entire time until I couldn't last another second of it; living in fear, never knowing when the next hit would be; not knowing if I would wake up in the morning each time I fell asleep beside this madman. And now it's the waiting. It is the knowing that each and every time I move, that he will find me. It is the torment of never being able to rest again. It is the torment in the knowledge that I will never again be able to feel completely safe.

I wish he would just kill me.

FIFTEEN

Fortunately, on this dark road, it is Shirley who finds me. Of all the people in this small town to drive past me this night, it is my landlord. Lovely, caring Shirley. So thankful am I that she recognised my car and pulled over. That she walked to the front of my vehicle and found me in a heap on the road, tears rolling down my face, vomit covering the bitumen beneath me. The panic attack subsided, but the emotional release still in full force. She didn't know what to make of my state, but her maternal instincts took over, and she helped me to her car.

She is thoughtful enough to find my bag, house keys, and phone. She locks my car and there it will stay on the side of the road. She knows her way around her house of course, first drawing a warm bath for me, then boiling the kettle and making the very best tea I have ever tasted. The warm comforting brew soothes my dry throat as I huddle under a blanket on the couch.

"Are you sure there isn't anyone I can call for you, my dear?" Shirley asks, possibly hoping for some sleep this evening but worried to leave me alone.

"I don't have anyone," I remind her.

I remember for the first time that night, my date with Samuel. Unable to contact him by phone, I imagine him waiting in the restaurant. I wonder how many times he tries to reach me. How many calls or texts would he send before giving up and leaving? Would he have ordered a drink? What would he have said to the wait staff about the failure of his date to arrive?

I feel awful. I have no idea how I will explain any of this to him, but I can't lie. If he is truly interested in being a part of my life, how can I not share with him my entire history? But, how can I? How unbelievable would it be for someone who doesn't yet know me to hear my story of torment from my ex-husband? And then it dawns on me. Each time I have seen my stalker, he has called me his wife. Does that mean the divorce didn't go through? Did he somehow manage to have it adjourned yet again? I don't want to imagine I am still married to that truly insane individual.

I see Shirley fading in the corner. She looks tired, and I offer her the spare room to rest for what is left of the night, but she insists on going home to sleep in her own bed. I don't blame her - there is nowhere better than home. *Home* - that word again. How he destroyed the meaning of that word for me tonight by offering to drive me home, which just confirms that he knows exactly where I live. Or was he suggesting he take me back to what was once our marital home? I don't want to imagine the meaning behind his words.

I lead Shirley to the door, give her a grateful hug and wish her good night. I wonder if she will be the last guest of the evening.

* * *

I somehow manage to fall asleep. The exhaustion on my body forces it into slumber not long before dawn. Staying up all night listening for noises in the house, keeping vigilant, keeping alert diminishes the final stores of energy I have left. Sleep in the end came quickly and soundly.

Early morning and I wake with a new determination to put an end to this rollercoaster that is my life. The leasing company is swift to send out someone to pick me up and take me back to my abandoned vehicle. I am most impressed that they agree to everything via email understanding that without a car or a phone, I have limited resources at hand. Once back on the road, thanks to a swift tyre change, I firstly head out to buy a new SIM card. How many of these I have purchased through the years is countless. Fortunately, I have no close family to speak of, as they would be frustrated with the number of times they would have to change my contact details in their phones.

The little family I have left in the world don't really bother keeping in contact. They all have their own lives and their own goals for their future and none of their plans involve me. They may have a long time ago. Prior to saying I do with Robert on our wedding day I was a regular to family events, but that changed on the wedding night. That was the last occasion I spent any real time with anyone I share DNA with. The last night as well that I was present with all of my family at the same time.

Who would have known on that day when my family came together to watch me promise myself to another, that life was about to change so dramatically for me? The isolation from my family started with inconvenient double bookings in our social calendar. My new husband needing me to be somewhere for his work or for his pleasure, always it seems on the same day as my family events. I was made to feel guilty for even considering abandoning him for a family function. And then over a very short time, it became more obvious, Robert forbidding me from seeing my family altogether. Telling me they were a bad influence on me. Insisting that they were coming between us. That seeing them would inevitably mean the death of our marriage.

Even my work became an issue for Robert. I thought I couldn't love him more, the day he encouraged me to give up my job to pursue my writing full time. I thought I was finally released from the burden of meaningless employment to become the creative I always wanted to be. But time proved this was just another ploy to further isolate me and keep me trapped financially by the man I had promised myself to.

I always wondered what a family might have done to change the dynamic between us. Loving a child or two would surely soften the man who had become so hard and bitter. But Robert insisted he wasn't quite ready to share me with a dependent child. He wanted more time together, just the two of us before we decided to spread our love to our children.

If any one of these events, triggered in me the realisation of what was to come, my life would look so very different now. And how could I have known otherwise. This was the man who promised to cherish me, to love me until death. He was the one person who should have always known what was in my best interests. I wanted to trust him. I thought I knew him so well when I married him but it turns out I knew nothing about him at all. Now all I know about this man is that he isn't giving up. He will continue to find me and torment me in this evil game of manipulation. This isn't going to stop, not unless I stop it for myself. I am the only person that I can rely on right now.

I make my way to the police station, hoping that Sergeant Thomas is on shift. Re-telling my unimaginable story again to another stranger would be beyond my capacity today. I park in the visitor car park, and make my way to the door. As previously, the small reception area is unmanned, so I press the bell on the counter. Sergeant Thomas is the first to answer my call for assistance, walking out through the glass sliding door with a smile on his face.

"Good morning Samara!" he greets me like an old friend, for which I am grateful.

"Um, good morning Sergeant, I mean…Thomas." I say, slightly unsure of how to address the officer now that we are on more familiar terms.

"How can I help you today?" he asks, skipping any idle chitchat to get to the formalities of his role.

I feel uncertain how to respond. All of a sudden, I am slightly embarrassed about why I am here. I stammer a little as I try to combine words together into a tangible sentence. "Um, I saw my stalker last night again."

Thomas doesn't immediately respond. I didn't imagine he would. He looks at me, unconvinced of the validity of my statement. I watch his expression, waiting for the muscles around his mouth to move to indicate the emergence of speech. He looks to the floor. "Are you here to make a statement?" He is suddenly all very businesslike.

Making a statement. I know exactly what that entails. I have made a dozen or more statements over the years, and not one of them has led to an arrest. Not one has even led to the beginnings of an investigation into my complaint. I don't want to waste my time, nor the Sergeant's. I don't want to be that woman who complains about nothing, only to find that when I really need police to attend they don't take me seriously. I decide to try my luck at the other objective I had in mind for today's visit to the station.

"No, I just wanted to let you know that I saw him again." I pause for a moment, to suggest a change of topic. "I really came down because I lost my phone, and I don't have Samuel's number anywhere, and I wondered if I could get it from you again."

The smile returns to his face when he realises the task at hand is much more straightforward than what I imagine he perceives as a wild goose chase for my imaginary stalker. He pulls his phone out of his back pocket, and begins the search for his friend's number. "Did you manage to have a lesson?" Thomas asks.

"Yes, I did. It was really good. It helped a lot with my confidence."

Thomas smiles a knowing smirk. "I thought it might." He looks at me directly now. "I had hoped you two would hit it off."

My turn to smirk now and blush as the officer in front of me, more perceptive than I gave him initial credit for, sees straight through my pretense.

He rattles off the number as I key it straight into my phone, making sure to save it straight to both my phone and my new sim.

"Now, don't go losing it again," Thomas orders me. "Sam is a very private person, and he doesn't give that number out lightly." A smile washes over his face again. For a moment, I imagine friendly dinners at Thomas's house. His wife hosting, several children running around loudly and Samuel and I exchanging glances in the madness that is their family home.

"I won't." I promise him.

Thanking him again, I enquire as to whether his wife liked the book. Some general small talk ensues about what I am currently working on, and whether I am planning on attending the big writer's conference coming at the end of the month.

"It's a big deal around here. As if we weren't busy enough with the movie sets scattered around and the extra security required for those. Now we have some writers' convention taking over the town, booking every last room left. We have to bring in extra officers from head office for the week," Thomas informs me.

I had completely forgotten about the convention. So busy dealing with my stalker, it had slipped my mind that Daniel is presenting and had asked me to come along for support. I make a mental note to check in on Daniel, and find out if he wants me to look over any of the presentation materials for him.

Right now, though, my priority is to apologise to Samuel for not making it to dinner last night. As soon as I am back in my car, having bid farewell to my new friend, Thomas, I dial Samuel's number. No answer. No ability to leave voice message either. So, I send a text.

Hi there!

I've hit send before I think to add anything more intelligible. With my nervousness on the increase at what I am going to say to Samuel, I decide it is best to explain myself in person. Hopefully I will do a better job at it than my embarrassing attempt at a text message. I check the time, and figure it is still early, so he might be at the studio rehearsing again.

I park in the studio car park designated for non-important visitors. The car park is for those who don't get immediate entry into the gate by a chauffeur driven limousine. I walk to the security barrier, and buzz for entry. The reply is quick and straight to the point. The security detail can see me from their post, but don't rise to greet me.

"Name?" the male voice demands over the speaker.

"Samara Sanders," I state firmly, as I had just days earlier on my first visit to the set.

"You are not on the list."

"Oh no, I'm not," I stumble over my words of explanation. I suddenly see that the security is more responsive than what I had assessed on my initial visit. "Um, I'm not on the list for today, but I was here two days ago."

The reply is again immediate and not for negotiation. "If you are not on the list, you are not gaining entry. Please return to your vehicle and leave the premises."

I stare straight at the security checkpoint, trying to make out the faces behind the dark glass giving them my best no nonsense stare. There is no point in debating. There is no one even listening to me anymore to argue the point with. I turn defeated and deflated, and head back to my car. From inside the vehicle, I pull my phone out of my bag once more and text again.

I tried to visit to explain but I can't get past security.

I don't feel as if I am doing well at explaining myself via text. I feel frustrated, and now slightly headachy. The heat of the season is just starting to rise, and I have yet to eat or drink anything besides my morning coffee. I decide to set off alone to the beach for a bite to eat.

* * *

Once at my beachside location, I grab a salad and a sparkling water and make my way onto the sand at my spiritual place. As always, I have a bag at the ready in the back of the car with the essentials for a beach visit. A sizeable towel, bikinis, a beach novel, sunscreen, a hat and a wrap being the entire contents of my large bag. I toss the bag over my shoulder, adding to it my mobile complete with new SIM card and my car keys. I double-check all the windows are up and the car is locked before heading down the wooden decking to my beach.

My spot under the tree is vacant. The entire beach is deserted, which is a welcome change to the busy film set that inhabited this tiny piece of paradise on my last visit. I am grateful for the quiet and solitude after the few crazy days I have endured. I place my bag on the sand and reef my towel out of it. Letting it open up with the breeze I watch it ride the current of air to spread out. Lowering it down, I immediately step onto it to hold it in place. I throw my bag onto one corner to secure it further. Leaning over I dig into the large blue carry-all to find my drink, and as I do I notice it.

For a moment, the skin on the back on my neck tingles with fear. My head immediately gets hot and my mind for an instant, falters, as the dizziness once more sets in. I stop myself. I close my eyes to imagine another image. I let out a deep breath. "It's not him." I say to myself. "It's not him." I repeat to convince myself even further. I continue my new ritual until the dizziness disappears and my head stops spinning. I take one last deep breath in and open my eyes again.

I look once more to the two wooden sticks beside me. Spliced together with what looks like twine, wedged deeply into the sand, in the protected safety from the weather just under my tree. The tree that for so many hours has provided me comfort during the hottest part of the day now harbours an alien object. A foreign entity designed I fear just for me. I reach over and with some force pull the wedged crucifix from its sandy resting spot. I turn the object over in my hands inspecting the piece for workmanship.

It is well constructed. Strong enough to withstand the elements but not too obviously engineered to be designed by a professional. The two pieces of wood, harvested from the surrounding bush land. The twine natural in colour, unobtrusive in nature and not naturally found on this shoreline. It doesn't appear to have been washed up with no sign of decay from the sea. The twine looks new. It is strong, the twine spliced so as to not require gluing or knotting. The end of the combined fragments burnt together to fuse for added durability.

I have seen this work before. I have witnessed Robert's hands splicing at the ropes that were to hold the sand anchor in place. I had received a lesson at the time. A rare gift from a genius that deemed most people unsuitable or unworthy to receive his precious time explaining the engineering feature of the splice. I know this is his work. I don't want to believe. I want to hope that a teenage boy has sat in this spot and fashioned the craft piece together but I can't convince myself of anything other than my stalker placing this souvenir here in this exact spot for me to find.

I hold the handmade cross in my hands. I look around to see if I can spot him watching me. I check the most obvious locations. I look out past the massive hill to my right. I check the place behind the sand dunes to my left. I search with my eyes beyond trees, on park benches on the hill behind me. I cannot see him squatting behind the huge rocks that protect the jagged shoreline. I see no sign of him, but feel him nevertheless. I stand up and hold the crucifix in the air, presenting first to the right, then to the left of where I stand.

I hold the object in front of me and ceremoniously snap the piece with my two hands. I hold the broken fragments of the sticks, one in each palm and present them again to my invisible stalker. I scream out into the vast space before me. I let the loud sound bellow from my throat. I throw my head back and project the noise into the atmosphere. When I am finished, I throw the two pieces of the broken cross behind me. They land at the base of the tree. I feel a strength I haven't known before.

I sit down and calmly find my salad in my bag and begin to eat. I giggle to myself for a second at my dramatic performance and feel thankful that I was absent of a public audience today. I have more than a vague idea of how insane that impromptu act must have looked to anyone seeing it. To anyone, that is, but the one person who it was intended for.

After I eat, I check my phone again for a reply from Samuel. I decide it wouldn't be out of the question to give him a quick phone call again. I press the green button to begin the call and wait with anticipation for his voice to respond. The phone rings out once more and I am left with no opportunity to leave a voice message. I feel deflated. Saddened that I haven't yet today had the chance to explain myself to Samuel. I can't imagine what must have been going through his mind last night when I didn't show.

The sun is tantalisingly warm on my skin. It is a familiar friend from a place and time that holds happy memories. I remember long summers in this very spot. Laughter and love abounded. Salty kisses, philosophical conversations about the future, and playful banter with my friends. This place, my spiritual home heals me in a way that none of my other locations have before. For a brief moment it holds that special place in my heart once more where anything is possible here. It gives me hope that a miracle can occur.

Magic happens in this place. Meeting Samuel, feeling that zing that I had imagined I had long lost the ability to feel with another. Cementing my friendship with Daniel. Sharing my darkest secrets, feeling trust in another again. Making new acquaintances in Thomas and Shirley and finding comfort in their support and belief in me.

For just the briefest of moments, I allow myself to imagine a life settled once more in a daily routine, free from looking over my shoulder. A life built around one place, a handful of trusted companions and the hope for love. I delude myself by envisioning a dream that is easy for others to turn into reality. For me, it will never be again. Not as long as my stalker can reach me. Not as long as he threatens my life. For as long as he is alive and hunting me I must keep running.

I let out the despair with a long exhale of my heated breath. The one small action makes me drowsy and I lay back, stretch my legs out in front of me and let my head rest gently on the towel beneath me. I close my eyes. Small moments of quiet sustain both the body and the soul.

* * *

My brain registers a shadow above me. A living presence moves past, blocking the sun's rays from my skin for just an instant. The amygdala, the part of my brain that governs senses reacts immediately sending my eyelids flying open for my sight to catch a glimpse of the intruding object. When my eyes focus, I see nothing. No plane in the sky, no tourist wandering past, no stalker that I can see. The brain plays an important role in regulating the entire body. Processing new information to categorise and store. Filing memories, some for easy retrieval, some locked away in a secured archive for more conscious recollection.

I sometimes wonder if my poor brain has been overworked. If it no longer is able to process, store and send messages, as it should. I wonder how it makes sense of nights like last night. I sometimes fear that my panic attacks are a result of my brain simply no longer coping with the years of stress it has had to endure. The large amounts of processing my trauma to continue to keep me alive must be wearing on the complicated organ that is the brain.

Long have I known the deception of the senses. The trickery that the five mechanisms of sensory intake play on the mind, seeing things in the dark, imagining smells and sounds that don't exist.

Feeling the ground beneath me suddenly disappear. Tasting life but not with the hunger I once knew. Taste in itself a strange concept. It has been a long time since I tasted something incredibly delicious. I fear the huge amount of cortisol that has pumped through my body during times of great stress has damaged my taste buds.

I sit and ponder the deception of the senses. If I can't trust my perception through the senses, how am I to decipher what is real and imagined. I think he knows that. I truly believe my stalker is relying on me doubting my own sanity. It is the ultimate manipulative play he holds over me.

But why he would continue to do this I do not understand. Why does he torture me like this? Why has he not just murdered me already?

SIXTEEN

Returning home, I pull into my driveway behind Shirley's car. I imagine she is here to check on me. She is such a lovely person - I truly got lucky this time with my choice of landlord. I quickly see she is not alone. Daniel is in the driveway with her, arms flailing about as if directing a scene on a movie set. Pointing to the house, then back to Shirley.

Curious as to what is going on, I park the car and walk toward the pair. Daniel is first to greet me with an exasperated sigh. "Can you please tell Shirley that she doesn't need to go to the expense of security systems? This is an outrage. And you can't expect her to be able to afford to do all of this for nothing."

I have no idea what Daniel is talking about, and begin my response with the forgotten pleasantries that he is normally so very fond of. "Good afternoon, Daniel. Hello, Shirley. How are you both today?"

"Exhausted darling!" Daniel is quick to respond. "I simply can't get through to Shirley here that she doesn't need to spend any more money on this house. She has done enough, and it simply does not offer her the return she needs to be able to spend anything more."

Daniel seems quite adamant that he has a clear case for a debate that is still absolutely foreign to me.

"Now, now, Daniel," Shirley begins in protest. "There is no need to worry about my finances. I will simply extend the credit card a little more. It is fine. I want to do this."

I fear I am falling even further behind, and need a more detailed explanation from one of them. "What exactly are we discussing here?

Daniel once more is the first to respond. "Shirley here wants to spend money she simply doesn't have on a security system to give you piece of mind about your supposed stalker."

He is unnecessarily flippant about the very real threat to my life. A little anger grows in me upon hearing his contempt. "I haven't asked Shirley to install anything for my benefit," I try to assure him.

"That's right. Samara hasn't asked for anything," Shirley agrees. "I simply want to do this for her. The poor thing can't sleep at night. She lives in constant fear for her life."

Daniel lets out a dramatic sigh as he rolls his eyes to the side. He drops his hands, letting them fall against his leg letting out a slapping sound as they hit the sides of his thighs. "Well, it is settled then. We do nothing." Daniel turns to walk toward the house. "Are you two coming? It's cocktail hour, my dears."

The win for Daniel is swift and non-negotiable but I see Shirley isn't satisfied. As Daniel strides towards the house, I step closer to Shirley. I can see the worry in her eyes. "Shirley, this is a lovely gesture, but Daniel is right. I absolutely do not want you spending any more money on the house for me."

"But dear…" She begins to protest. "What about your ex-husband" She asks. "What if he comes back? I'm worried for you all alone here. What if something happens to you? I wouldn't be able to live with myself."

My heart warms at the sight of this gorgeous woman in front of me, a beautiful soul who truly cares about my wellbeing and maybe one of the few people who actually seems to believe the details of the horror story that is my life.

"Please, Shirley. I beg you. I don't want you to do anything. I have this handled. Trust me. Everything will be fine." I promise her.

She resigns finally to defeat, and gives me a loving hug as she says farewell. I thank her again for her concern, and suggest a catch up for dinner sometime in the coming week - my small way of saying thank you for all the care she has shown. I wave goodbye as Shirley pulls her car into the street, giving her horn a little sound as she drives away.

I take a deep breath and turn to face the house. Daniel is no doubt already inside, stirring up a heady mix of alcohol and ice. I could use the distraction to be honest, but that still doesn't forgive Daniel's very minimising view of my fear for my life. I walk toward the house, not bothering to park my car inside. I make a note to come back and put it away later.

Once near the entry, I hear the music blaring. The cheerful tones of what I imagine to be an Australian eighties pop starlet sound through the speaker. He really is caught in an awful time warp, our Daniel. I barely make the few steps through the door before the glass is thrust into my hand. Pink and sparkly, the liquid looks enticing. I have no idea what Daniel has found in my kitchen to conjure up such a delicacy, but I am grateful for the refreshing sensation in my mouth. I take another sip before Daniel slaps my hand.

"How dare you! We haven't toasted yet!" His voice is shrill, matching in part the vocals resonating from the Bluetooth speaker in the lounge area.

"I am not sure what I have to toast to at the moment." My mood is melancholy at best.

"We are toasting to your new boyfriend, aren't we? How did he handle being stood up last night? Did you make it up to him with a good blowie today?"

I nearly choke on my next mouthful of cocktail as Daniel's words leave his lips. Part of me wants to laugh at his crassness, but part of me wants to slap him for suggesting I am that carefree with my sexuality that I would provide oral sex by way of apology. But before I respond, I am reminded that I am yet to hear back from Samuel. Two phone calls and two text messages later, and still not a single word in reply from him. I fear he may be too angry with me to forgive me for failing to show for our date.

"Actually," I begin to explain to my friend. "I haven't heard back from him. I don't think he wants to see me again. He isn't responding."

"Well, that's fortunate for you anyway. These actors are simply useless in bed, my darling. They have no idea which way is up or down. And seriously, they are just dead fish. They save all of their sexual tension for their acting. What you see on the big screen, darling, does not translate into real life. And trust me, I have had many!"

I am not shocked by Daniel's evaluation of the sexual prowess of the acting community. Nor am I surprised by his flippant remark regarding many lovers. I had gathered from the little I know of Daniel already that he has lived quite a life. Taking lovers as he wishes, discarding them just as quickly. Utilising people to fulfill his many sexual desires. His appetite for new flesh is insatiable. Experimenting with their bodies then sending them away when he is finished as if he is throwing away a coffee cup once the vessel is emptied of its usefulness.

I had heard this same thing said about all creative people. Inspired by the spotlight, turning on the charm when networking and all the attention is on them but then in the privacy of their own homes, dark and brooding. Insular, wanting to spend time alone when not working, so drained from using every ounce of their energy for their craft. But in my limited experience I have found the exact opposite to be true. Creative souls can be the most romantic, the most open minded and loving. As they are used to expressing their feelings through their art, they feel comfortable to show affection and share emotions.

Not that I think I will ever get the chance to find out firsthand with Samuel. Not hearing back from him seems to me to be a sure sign that he has lost interest after our failed attempt at a dinner date.

"My darling, you aren't still brooding over that pretty boy actor, are you?" Daniel never holds back on telling me exactly what he thinks.

"No!" I am quick to snap back my reply. Of course, that is exactly what I am doing, and Daniel knows it.

"You know what you need, my dear?" His words are less harsh now, and suggestive in nature.

"What?" I ask him with reluctance. I tilt my head to the side knowing I might not really need to hear the answer but ask the question anyway.

"You need to fuck someone!" Daniel announces this like it is the answer to the meaning of life.

"Really now?" I decide to play along, thinking I may already know what the next part of the suggestion is.

"Yes, of course. The quickest way to get over someone is to get under somebody else." Daniel doesn't give much away about how I might go ahead and do this.

"Do you know who might be able to help me do that?" I ask, toying with my writer friend.

"Well, I would love to darling, but I am otherwise engaged at the moment."

"What?" I sputter the words, not entirely happy to be feeling rejected by the most sexually active and carefree man I think I have ever met. I look to him, wondering what the throw away comment could mean. I hope Daniel will be forthcoming with a response. I need further explanation as to why all of a sudden Daniel has decided to be otherwise engaged at the moment. He looks at me and sees me staring in his direction. I raise one eyebrow encouraging him to go into more detail.

"Oh darling, don't be upset with me. It's just you are not really my type." He answers with a lack of empathy for my current emotional state.

"Oh, I see…" I don't really understand, but am happy to say anything to put an end to this awkward conversation. A welcome change of mood comes in the form of a distracting idea. "How about we do some work on our book?" I suggest hoping this will keep us occupied and my mind busy for a few hours.

"Oh, that sounds like work, sweet, and I'm not at all up to working today." Daniel searches through his pocket, pulling out a small USB stick. "But I do have something you might want to see."

I have no idea what could be on the stick, but as always, I give in to Daniel and whatever scheme he has in mind for the day.

"So, what is it?"

"It's your boy. In some low budget, locally made, cinematic disaster."

I am blown away. Daniel really does care. Through all the bravado and insensitivity to my emotional state, he really does think of me. I feel honoured, and more than just a little excited to see Samuel's work. I had barely even had the chance to do any real cyber stalking, but Daniel obviously has, even going so far as to find a way to download his movie.

"OK, you get the drinks. I'll get the snacks, and meet you on the lounge." I have a new bounce in my step, and a keen desire to spend some quality time staring at the man that I have more than a little liking for, even if it is just on the screen.

SEVENTEEN

Daniel's initial foreboding of the movie is fairly accurate. The script itself is cringe worthy. The plot is absent for the most part. The dynamic between the lead characters is only slightly believable. But then there is Samuel. He looks absolutely gorgeous. It's a shame I'm seeing him for the first time with his shirt off in digital format rather than in person, but it is worth every second of filming.

It is obvious he is doing his own stunt work. I can make out moves that are typically his just from the small time I had already spent with him in training. The strong purposeful blows are mesmerising to watch. The action-packed film has just the right amount of street fighting for me to watch without getting completely bored. But things are starting to look up. It appears as if a love scene may be on the cards, and I watch my Samuel lean in for his first kiss with his opposite lead.

I squirm in my seat a little to be on the edge of the lounge. I am about to watch what I had hoped would happen in real time for me one day. But alas, it now seems as if I will have to just be content with watching him kiss another. The scene heats up rather quickly, just as I imagine it would with anyone feeling the electricity that radiates from this man. I think the female lead has forgotten she is in front of the camera altogether, as her acting until this particular point had left a lot to be desired and this is her first believable scene yet.

Just as his jeans are about to come off, the doorbell rings. I pretend for a second that I don't hear it, hoping Daniel might get up and answer it. He hears it too, and responds by increasing the volume of the television to try to drown out the unwelcome intrusion to our viewing. I look at him, and he is entranced as well. This star has obvious appeal to both sexes.

The visitor persists, and the doorbell rings once more followed shortly after by a double knock. I sigh and wait for a second, hoping again that Daniel responds. He isn't moving anywhere. I stand up to walk toward the front entry. "Pause it Daniel!" I demand but he doesn't respond. Instead, he sits with his eyes glued to the screen as our star allows his romantic interest to unzip his jeans. "Daniel, pause!" I yell louder this time. I am not going to miss a second of this, and I know trying to talk Daniel into replaying what I miss will be a battle of wills.

Finally, he obliges and hits the pause button. The scene is frozen in time. The female lead has her hands on his zipper while Samuel is looking down at her on her knees in front of him. I stop to look at the screen one more time before forcing myself to make my way to the door to my uninvited intruder. I open the door, only giving it a fragment of my attention as I keep an ear out for Daniel to hear if he restarts the movie without me. "Get us another drink!" I yell back to him, in the hope that it will keep him from sneakily pressing play in my absence.

The door is open, and I finally turn my full attention to my guest. "I'll have one too if I am being invited in."

The smooth voice, the flirty suggestion, the gorgeous blue eyes force my heart to pound through my chest. He doesn't hesitate to enter the front door without an invite, and pauses for an instant as he kisses my cheek. My face burns with heat from the intensity of the touch. "Samuel!" I finally manage to utter his name. It seems surreal to see him in person again. "You are here." I am lost for words.

"I hope that's OK." Samuel responds.

I am vaguely aware of Daniel still in the room next to me, and the very real introduction of the two men that is now going to have to happen. I just hope Daniel can be polite. "Of course. I am happy to see you again."

"I was hoping you would say that." Samuel smiles, and those blue eyes reach straight into my soul.

I begin to walk Samuel from the front entry when I hear it. Daniel has pressed play on the movie, just as I had expected him to do. The sound of the booming male voice from the stereo system is familiar to not only me, but to my new guest. He stops mid step and looks to me, shooting me a knowing smile as he quickens his pace to walk toward the offending sound. He stops as soon as his eyes find the screen and he views himself right there in front of us all.

"Oh, my Goodness!" Daniel shrieks from the kitchen bench as soon as he recognises our guest. He looks towards Samuel, and back to the screen. He throws his head back, and laughs a raucous laugh that he quickly loses control of. "Oh, this is awkward for you, darling." He finds my humiliation yet again a matter of unquantifiable amusement.

Samuel raises his hand in greeting to Daniel, then turns back to address me. "Are you enjoying it?" he muses flirtatiously with me.

I am beyond embarrassment. I look to the television again and see Samuel's naked butt in full frame on the screen. His muscular shoulders moving rhythmically as his hands instruct the mouth of the female lead as she concentrates on pleasuring him. I look to Samuel once more, then drop my eyes to the ground. I wish for a moment it would swallow me whole. I cannot believe this is happening to me.

"She just replays this one scene over and over again," Daniel lies to Samuel.

Samuel smiles a little in reply. Not needing to ask more.

"He's lying about that." I attempt to clarify.

Daniel is beside us now as he passes Samuel a martini glass of something without looking at him. His eyes are locked on the screen. I glance to the kitchen, where my drink is left on the counter. Daniel and Samuel stand their ground behind the lounge, both watching the screen as I make my way over to the kitchen, grab my glass, and swallow it in one swift movement. The scene is playing out on the large screen in the centre of the room. Samuel is now on top of the naked female lead, writhing away, his groin moving up and down, as he is lost in the sexual tension of the moment. I put my head in my hands and close my eyes. No words are spoken. The vocals from the film fill the void between my male companions and myself.

The female lead screams out in ecstasy as Samuel drops in a heap on top of her. He too obviously completely satisfied by the sexual escapade. The scene fades, and the landscape of the vast isolated outback becomes the focus.

Daniel doesn't skip a beat as he turns to Samuel beside him. "I thought you would be taller in person."

"Yeah, I get that a lot," Samuel replies undeterred by the remark. His friendly nature and obvious self-confidence ensures he isn't easily offended. "I'm Samuel, by the way." He offers Daniel his hand in welcome.

Daniel offers a limp shake, obviously not awe struck in the presence of this screen god. "Yes, I am well aware."

"Daniel!" I yell across the room to get his attention. "Can I have another please?" I beg him offering up my empty glass as evidence that I require his assistance.

Daniel responds and walks towards me. "Lush!" he utters loud enough for both of us to hear him.

As Daniel mixes his liquid experiment, I walk back toward Samuel. He is smiling at me as I cross the room. Any embarrassment at what he has walked into is not apparent by this complete sense of ease as he sips on his drink. I sense a moment of nervousness as he begins to speak. "I was hoping I could speak to you," he half whispers, apparently hoping to not be overheard.

"Of course. Shall we talk on the deck?" I needlessly point in the direction of the large outdoor area.

"There is no need to whisper. Anything you say to her, she will just repeat to me the minute you have left," Daniel calls from the kitchen.

"Daniel!" I yell back at him.

"That is not true!" I direct my reassurance to Samuel. I try my best to believe myself. That certainly may have been the case prior to meeting Samuel, but not now. Not if I believe I have the chance of something real and serious with this stunning actor. I only hope that is what he has come here to tell me.

Daniel doesn't stop. He offers an explanation to Samuel as to our relationship. "It's OK. I am her gay bestie. We tell each other everything." He pauses before adding quite unnecessarily, "I mean, we have fucked once mind you, but you know, it was just for something to do."

"Daniel!" I yell louder this time.

I grab Samuel by the arm to try to encourage a faster pace. As soon as we are outside, I close the large sliding door, offering at least some form of privacy. "I can explain."

"There is no need. I do not need to know any more than what I just heard." He smiles a reassuring smile at me and I am instantly put at ease once more. "I hope I am not intruding."

"Of course not. I have been trying to reach you. I was worried you were mad at me."

"I was a little surprised when you didn't show up, but then I heard what had happened and I wanted to come and check on you and make sure you were OK." He pauses, looks down at the ground and then into my eyes. "And I hoped that we could try again. For dinner, tonight, if you are free." He looks at me hopefully.

"I would love that." I smile back at him. I cannot believe how fortunate I am to have met this man. Not only is this amazing creature here in the flesh but he is making it obvious that he too feels some connection that he wants to explore. "Do you want to stay and watch the rest of the movie?"

"Will that be alright with your friend?" He is thoughtful and aware that he has arrived uninvited.

I don't hesitate to respond. "If it's not, I will Kung-Fu kick his butt straight out of here."

He laughs at my pitiful attempt at humour, but I am happy the situation can have a moment of lightness. I begin to make my way back in the house, hoping that I am not about to have another naked bottom scene to contend with.

Then a thought hit me. I turn to Samuel. "By the way, how did you know that I got a flat tyre last night and couldn't ring you?"

He looks a little sheepish. Not fully certain if he wants to divulge his secret with me. "When I couldn't reach you by phone, I contacted Thomas to see if he had heard anything. He said that Shirley had been to see him and told him the whole story." He stops before adding more. "That is also how I got your address. I hope you don't mind."

"Wow!" I exclaim. "I forgot what it was like to live in such a small town." My mind wanders to what other gossip might be flying around about me. I don't dare think about it a moment longer. I am just grateful that he is here now and wanting to spend some time with me. I am not entirely sure how Daniel will take the news that we will be entertaining a guest for the afternoon, but he will just have to deal with it as best Daniel can.

We enter the lounge room again, and Daniel is back on the lounge, having started the movie again without us. Samuel is once more the star of the scene, fighting his way through a particularly violent brawl with his arch nemesis. "Daniel, move over," I order him so he will make room for Samuel and I.

"OK, OK, wouldn't want your little boyfriend here to get violent or anything."

Daniel's jealousy that he isn't the centre of attention is evident as he offers up the sarcastic remark, shuffling over just enough for us to squeeze onto the couch beside him. I am too embarrassed by the reference to the term boyfriend to meet Samuel's eyes, but I can tell he is staring intently at me. I glance quickly, and catch his smile. He puckers his lips and sends me an air kiss. He appears quite pleased with himself, and completely comfortable with the quickly established label to our relationship.

EIGHTEEN

An afternoon of downloaded Samuel movies, far too many cocktails and freshly delivered pizzas has resulted in a less than active few hours. Night has fallen and Daniel begins to make his way to the door.

"You are not driving Daniel!" I order him. "Stay the night in the spare room."

"And listen to you two making noisy heterosexual love all night? No, thank you, my sweet." Daniel can become more than a little catty when he wants to. "I have a lift anyway, thank you very much. I have my very own little toy boy waiting for me."

It is of no surprise that Daniel has failed to mention anyone in particular that he is seeing. He does keep some things very private. I wonder if this means he has some emotional connection to this particular person, being that he doesn't seem to want to share any details with me.

He kisses me on the cheek, and shakes Samuel's hand unconvincingly, unable to hide his contempt for my new companion. I watch him as he closes the front door, and run to the window to see if I can catch a glimpse of the mysterious driver coming to collect him. I watch as he walks down the drive and stops in front of a black sedan.

The dark windows and lack of decent street lighting prevents me from seeing anything more, the cars bonnet the only visible clue from my position in the window. Hidden behind the neighbouring trees, it would almost appear as if the driver wants to remain a mystery. Or knowing Daniel, as I do, the driver was most likely instructed to remain inconspicuous.

I turn back to Samuel still seated on the couch. Arms outstretched above him. A yawn escapes his mouth and he is comfortable enough around me to not bother to hide it with his hand. "I must be getting going too," he offers but I don't believe him.

"Do you have somewhere to be?" I enquire.

"Not at all. I just thought you might need to get some sleep."

"You can stay in the guest room if you like. It's probably not a good idea to drive after those cocktails," I offer, hoping that this will provide me just a bit more time with this beautiful individual.

"Sure, thanks. Which way is it to the spare room?" he asks, suddenly rising from the lounge.

"Um, it is the third door down the hall," I offer, but secretly hope he doesn't immediately retreat. Another hour at least would be perfect before I lose him to slumber, though I dare not offer. I figure he has been working long hours on set so probably needs the rest.

He turns to me, and throws his arms around me. It is quite unexpected, but very much welcome. He kisses my forehead and bids me goodnight. "Sweet dreams," he whispers before releasing me from his warm embrace and heads into the bedroom.

I stand for a moment, and hear the door close. He is gone. Already, after only a moment alone since Daniel's departure, he is gone. I now won't get to see him again until the sun rises above the horizon.

I walk around and turn off the lights. I pad quietly down the hall so as not to wake my guest, and close my bedroom door behind me. As I walk into my bathroom, I smile, knowing that the most gorgeous man is a mere few feet away from me. I begin to brush my teeth, checking out my reflection in the mirror as I do. My mind takes me back to my special guest, and I try to imagine what he might be wearing. I wonder if he sleeps in his underwear, or in nothing at all. I feel the heat rush to my face again at the thought of it.

I splash some cold water on my face, then walk to the bed, discarding my clothes as I pull my blanket back to crawl into my soft comfortable mattress. I stretch, and then roll over on to my side, taking my pillow with me as I do. I give it a little squeeze, imagining for a minute it is Samuel. My bare nipples harden now at the thought of him. I close my eyes, and his face is the only image in front of me. His smile, his bright beaming eyes scorching into mine. He has no idea the effect he has on me. I roll onto my back, and let out a massive sigh. How hard is this going to be to try to sleep with Samuel so close?

A tingle works its way through my body, and my nakedness beneath the sheet becomes obvious, as my skin is alert to touch. I can't bare the heaviness of the linen on top of me, so grab the corner and throw the offending material across the bed. The suddenness of the night air on my delicate skin ignites my senses. I have but one thought racing through my mind.

Before I have time to stop myself, my feet have found the floor. My hand is on the door handle, and I am in the hallway. I don't falter. I walk directly to my guest bedroom and without knocking, open the door slightly. I look for any sign of life on the mattress in the centre of the room. There is a slight shuffle beneath the sheets. It is difficult to see if he is still awake. I step inside the room, and close the door behind me.

I tiptoe the few steps to the side of the bed. I reach for the cover and pull it open just slightly enough to crawl in beside my houseguest. I hear him take a deep breath. I feel his hand on my stomach. I lay flat on my back, suddenly nervous for what I have started. His hand moves to my breast, his mouth finds my neck, and he instantly begins to tickle the sensitive area with his tongue. His body leaves the mattress, and is held beside me, allowing his hand full access to my body.

He searches it frantically, every inch of skin skimmed over, with no surface left unexplored. He moves his body on top of mine. The dim light from the moon radiating through the window catches the wicked glimmer in his eye as his mouth finds mine again. His lips push down onto mine parting for his tongue to now explore my mouth. I run my hands across his naked torso, and settle them on his bare behind. I give a gentle squeeze, and his erection hardens more as I push him into me. He lets out a moan, satisfied that he has understood my request as he pushes his leg between mine and pries them apart. His body needs no directions.

His hardness finds the moist place between my legs, and he enters me. My head is automatically thrown back against the pillow as the beautiful agony of him inside me takes control over my body. He pushes further into me, taking a moment to watch my face as I bite my lower lip in pure pleasure. Ensured of my enjoyment, he withdraws just that little too far, waiting for a second before thrusting inside me once more. I let out a loud moan, and I see him smile. He enjoys watching my response, and is turned on by my pleasure.

His strong arms hold his body above me. I turn, and bite into his bicep as once more he pushes his erection inside me. My legs lift in the air to allow him every access he needs. He leans down, and finds my mouth again, and his pace speeds up as our mouths explore each other's. He once more returns to my neck, travelling down to my breast, his lips find my nipple. Hard in his mouth, he suckles the delicate area. His teeth brush slightly across it, not faltering his rhythm at all. He slows down once more.

Biting a little harder, he listens for my sounds. My moan pierces through the silent night. He speeds up. His erection finds the perfect balance of pace and depth. He doesn't stop, and I feel my body heighten and fall in a breathtaking orgasm. He slows, and looks into my eyes, the pulsing of my body on his hardness evidence that my climax continues.

He kisses my lips - more gently this time. He pulls his face away, and his eyes meet mine once more. His radiant smile beams down on me. He is obviously pleased with his performance - the result he was hoping for coming quickly and with little effort on my behalf. "Again?" He flirts with me.

I bite my bottom lip, and cannot find the words to respond. I simply nod my head in agreement. His body comes to life once more, and the rhythm we find is effortless as if we were always meant to be together.

NINETEEN

The sun blasts through the bedroom window, the birds are chirping, and my eyes open to the brightest of days. I immediately remember the night before, and roll over to throw my arm across my bedmate. But it is empty. Samuel isn't there. I am instantly deflated, as I imagine him waking early this morning, quietly gathering his things so as not to wake me, and making his exit from the house.

I run my hand across the linen that housed his body just a short time earlier. I take a deep breath, and ignite my nostrils with his scent. I instantly go to that place of regret. Knowing I instigated a wild night of passion maybe just a little too early in our fledging relationship. I can only imagine what he thinks of me. I mean if I was so quick to jump into bed with him, he must only imagine I am like that with every man I date. How is he to know any different, especially after Daniel let slip the unfortunate secret that I had in fact slept with him as well?

And the truth couldn't be more different. Before Daniel and our night of sexual release, I hadn't slept with another man since my ex-husband. I haven't even thought about it. So consumed I have been with running and hiding, I haven't let anyone else get this close to me before. If I was honest with myself, the real truth is that I had long lost any desire for intimacy with anyone.

So foreign has the thought been of making love with someone that I had almost forgotten what it was like to be close to another. Until Daniel, of course, and his reminder about how good it feels to be intimate with someone, though that failed to compare in any way to last night. Lovemaking with Samuel was spiritual. It wasn't just two people having sex. It felt like two people finding each other, knowing this was how it was meant to be all along.

I sigh as I remember his touch, and feel dread that I may have lost it just as quickly as I found it. I roll onto my back, and drop my arms stretched out to either side of me. I listen for the birds, eager for their morning feed, and I start to crave a hot brewed coffee. The smell almost too real, I imagine the enticing aroma waft through the house. Footsteps appear down the hall and my first reaction is to panic. As I allow it to subside, I listen further to hear the clanging together of plates.

Samuel enters the guest bedroom, meekly carrying a wooden tray of breakfast delicacies. I see the food before I look to him – a pot of steaming hot coffee; fresh bagels, toasted with a side of jam and a side of cream cheese; strawberries cut in halves and a small glass jar with a freshly picked flower from the garden. Quite a cliché for a breakfast in bed but a feast to the eyes neither the less.

I turn my attention to Samuel as I sit up in bed, covering my modesty with the sheet. I need not have bothered, as Samuel is clearly not at all shy. His naked body is toned, tanned and erect, and he notices my stare move down his body to his hardness. "I am sorry, you just have this effect on me."

"No need to apologise at all," I assure him

He puts the tray carefully on the base of the bed, and leans down to kiss my mouth. "Good morning, by the way, my creative goddess."

"Creative goddess?" I giggle as I repeat his overly generous compliment.

"You are. I have just been reading your work." His head tilts to indicate the book placed on the side of the tray he carried into the bedroom. He has with him a romantic novel bordering on erotica. Not my best work, but my first foray into the more, steamy sex scenes, something I had never felt overly confident writing.

"Pretty sexy, by the way." His smile widens, and I swear I see his erection grow. He catches my eye and covers himself casually with one hand. His other hand is signaling for me to look upward. "My face is up here by the way." He laughs, for the effect he has on me is obvious, and he appears to enjoy the power he can hold over me.

He crawls into bed, sits upright and pulls the tray to his lap. "I insist you eat first before we begin round two." He picks up a strawberry, and places it gently into my mouth. My lips part for him, allowing him again full access. He is casual, playful, and light. There is no awkwardness between us that can sometimes come with the morning after revelations following the first-time having sex.

He pours a coffee. "How do you have it?" He has thought of everything. A small amount of sugar and a jug of milk are at the ready to suit any order I may request of him.

"Just black please." He hands the cup to me and begins to pour his own. Black as well - no sugar, no milk. Coffee just as it was intended to be.

He balances the cup carefully on the tray and gets to work on the bagels. "Jam or cream cheese?"

I lick my lips, suddenly ravenously hungry. I now understand why Samuel insisted we eat. "Mmm...jam, I think. Something sweet and sticky." Just as the knife is about to dive into the delicious preserve, the bagel in his other hand ready for the coating of the smooth spread, his smile widens. I can only guess he has enjoyed the same wicked thought as me.

He spreads the bagel and puts the knife down on the tray. He leans towards me, and feeds me the warm pastry. He watches me bite into it. I keep my eyes transfixed on his as I chew and swallow the delicious mouthful. I put my mouth to the bagel once more, but instead of biting, I gently lick some of the sweet preserve with my tongue. He closes his eyes for a second, and his smile spreads across his face even more. He is putty in my hands, as I am in his.

I bite into the bagel once more, and then take it from his hand to offer for him to take a bite. He bites hard into the soft dough, making a mess of the jam and getting it across both corners of his mouth. He chews, and allows his tongue to lick the sticky substance from the corner of his mouth. I watch, not taking my eyes off his gorgeous face for a second. He is breathtaking to watch. I can't stand it anymore, and I move onto my knees so I can lean over and lick the last remnants of preserve from his mouth.

Instinctively, I know he feels the same as he lifts the tray and places it on the floor beside him. His hands grab me by the hips and lowers me on top of him. My body knows what to do next, and as he enters me once more, I let out a light moan with intense pleasure I have never felt before. We have all the time in the world, and our lovemaking is slow and sensual. He is quiet, as I am, for there is no need for words. We both sense what the other wants. Afterwards, I fall asleep on his chest. The strong sunlight is streaming through the windows. The coffee is now cold, the breakfast tray long forgotten. We stay like this for a long time, neither of us wanting to leave the embrace that feels like home.

It is lunchtime by the time we find ourselves in the kitchen. Starving for nourishment that is not of the flesh, we search the fridge for something to eat. "You don't have much here." He announces. The disappointment in his voice is difficult not to notice. "How about I take you out to lunch?" He offers, a lighter tone suddenly to his voice as the idea takes hold.

"Sure." I respond. I am uncertain why I am not jumping at the chance of spending more time with this godlike creature. I feel a little hesitant given the current state of affairs to be seen in public with Samuel. It is not that I wouldn't love to be with him but I do fear the emergence of my stalker at any time. And I have no doubt he watches me from afar when I am in public. He will be careful to hide himself from view so as to be able to watch from a safe distance. He will hide in the shadows, to see, but not to be seen.

We dress and Samuel offers to take his car. We drive immediately to the beach and spot a little café by the water. We feast, suddenly hungrier than we imagined we could be. Our conversation is light and effortless. The smiles are impossible to wipe from our satisfied faces. I imagine it would be obvious to anyone watching that we are more than a little besotted with one another. His hand barely leaves my side, resting on my thigh, holding my hand or touching my face to remove a stray hair the ocean breeze has blown across my mouth.

He looks not at me but into me. I can't stop staring. His smile is absolutely hypnotising. I cannot believe I have fallen for this man so quickly. It scares me to think about it. How much has changed in just a few hours. Yesterday, unable to reach him and not thinking I would ever see him again. I was certain that I had ruined any chance of getting to know this amazingly creative genius. And today, less than twenty-four hours later and I can't imagine not having him in my life.

I had heard of love at first sight and even written about it in my romance novels, never for a second believing it was something that happened to real people. Until now that is. Until, it was, meeting Samuel for that very first time, and that zing. That first electrifying touch and somehow, I knew this thing we had was something special.

TWENTY

"I might have to say goodbye for a while. I have a couple of meetings this afternoon that I must attend. If there was any way to get out of them, I swear, I would," Samuel announces.

"Oh, no, that's perfectly understandable," I respond knowing full well that I have a mound of work to do myself. Writing isn't just a hobby for me now. I have contractual obligations to complete my current work before the end of the year, and with the Daniel distractions and the stalker setbacks, I have fallen more than a little behind. Not to mention, it is hard to be creative when fearing for my life.

We head back to Samuel's car and as we drive along the beach, I see Daniel's house. "Samuel, could you drop me off here?" I suggest.

"Of course." He slows the car and pulls to the side of the road. "Who lives here can I ask?"

"Daniel." I am a little reluctant to say. "I thought I would check on him and maybe see if he is ready to do some work today on our book. He has been preoccupied lately, and we are losing momentum."

"Do you want me to wait to make sure he is home? It looks a little locked up."

"No, I am sure he will be home, and besides, the walk back to my house isn't all that far if he isn't."

Samuel reluctantly kisses me goodbye, a lingering kiss that is difficult to extract myself from. He catches my eyes and my complete attention as he speaks. "I'll see you soon."

I nod in the positive, somewhat speechless at the thought of seeing him again. I give him one more kiss, and put my hand on the door handle.

"Is this going to be debriefing with your friend about last night?" he smiles as he asks me. Not appearing at all concerned, just curious as to the real nature of the visit.

I have been caught out. It is as if Samuel can read my mind. "Um, maybe a little," I admit. "But I promise no details!"

"I don't mind at all. That's what friends do."

I lean over again for one last kiss on his lips. I am addicted already. Barely able to leave this man's presence, it is difficult for me to actually step out of the car. One final kiss is not enough, but I remind myself silently that I will see him again soon, and I finally exit the vehicle. I smile and wave as I watch him drive away. I turn and walk up the drive to Daniel's house. Samuel was right. It does look remarkably quiet. There is no noise coming from the house. Most of the doors and windows appear closed. There is no telltale sign of life inside.

I walk to the front door and ring the intercom. I know there is a camera capturing my every move, so poke out my tongue for Daniel to get a warm welcome from me. I wait and hear nothing. No response. No opening door. I walk to the garage, and hop on tiptoes to look through the small window at the side of the luxury mansion. Daniel's car is there. Locked and secured.

I remember the night before and Daniel hopping into the stranger's vehicle. Well, not a stranger to Daniel obviously, but a mystery man, details of whom unknown to me at least. I wonder if Daniel has spent the night at his companion's house. And I remember him telling me that he will happily have sex at someone else's house, but then he quickly has to return home to sleep soundly on his own in his own bed – a little quirk I guess he has, which I understand. Sleeping with someone can take a bit of getting used to - except for Samuel, of course. My sleep last night was one of the most sound and peaceful slumbers I have had in a long time.

I return to Daniel's front door, adamant I won't give up. He must be inside there somewhere. Daniel is not an outdoorsy kind of person, so wouldn't travel anywhere by foot, for fears the damage the sun could inflict upon his boyish looks. If he doesn't drive somewhere, he doesn't go at all. He must be inside. I push the intercom again, this time reserving the right for funny faces until I check on Daniel's current mood. There is the possibility he is extremely hung-over or ill, and is not responding to the door quickly.

I press once more on the silver button, holding it just a second too long. This will be my final attempt, and if Daniel doesn't answer I will make my way home by foot to, as promised, continue my own writing for the afternoon. I wait, and then silently count to ten, more of a way of forcing myself to leave than anything else. I really want to see Daniel this morning, and the mystery of his silence has got me more than a little intrigued.

I count to ten, and as the strategy requires, turn to walk away. Just then, the click of the lock sounds, and the door slowly opens. Daniel is hidden mostly behind the door, his face looking toward the ground. My assumption appears correct. Daniel looks hung-over. I step into the entrance, pushing the door open as I do. I begin to speak. "Well, that took forever. Looks like you've had a good night than."

Daniel doesn't speak, but merely takes a step backwards to allow me to enter. He closes the door, and finally looks up at me. Daniel's face is bloodied and bruised. His right eye bright red from a burst blood vessel. His bottom lip is split, dried blood filling the crevice of the rough surface. He says nothing, giving me time to take in the frightful sight in front of me.

"Daniel…" I grab his hands, and he shrieks, the pain obvious with the sudden movement. "What happened to you? Who did this?"

He looks to the floor again, yet to say a single word in reply. The shame on his face is apparent, as if he himself caused this. "Daniel, answer me. What happened?"

He looks up at me once more. "It's nothing." His tone is flat.

I take him gently by the hand, and manoeuvre him to the lounge. I sit and he follows. "Let me see you." I examine the multiple wounds cringing as I look closer at them. His face is swollen, and his eye looks like it is about to pop out of the socket. He has cuts that look like they could use a stitch or two. "We need to get you to the hospital."

"No." He is quick to respond. "I don't need a hospital." He is sure of his intent. His response leaves little room for negotiation.

I pause and try to imagine what he must be feeling. I don't need to use my writer's imagination for I know this feeling all too well - the guilt at allowing the injuries to occur to; whatever dangerous situation he put himself into; whatever words he said to ignite a fight; whatever behaviour he did or didn't do; the shame at facing the world like this is devastating. It would be obvious to all that see him, that he was in a situation with another and that he allowed this to happen. He couldn't or wouldn't defend himself. He was prey to another. Not a stranger, possibly a lover. He was beaten and abused by someone he trusted.

"Daniel, I understand how you must feel. You know I have been there too." I want him to know that he has no reason to feel judged, for I, of all people know too well the shame and embarrassment that he must be feeling right now. "I understand how this has happened, and it isn't your fault."

Daniel jumps to his feet. "Oh, for fuck's sake, don't make this about you!" he screams at me. His sudden anger completely out of character for my easygoing friend.

"I am sorry. I didn't mean to presume anything, Daniel. Please, I am just worried about you. Please tell me what happened."

"It's nothing. Just a little energetic foreplay gone a bit wrong."

"Daniel." I stop, barely knowing what to say next. "This isn't just rough sex. This is assault. This is a crime. You need to go to police. Tell them what has happened. You need medical attention for some of those cuts."

"You don't understand. This is different. For God's sake this isn't about you. Stop making this all about you." Daniel's tone is serious as he speaks.

I hardly know how to respond. I am unsure where this directed anger is coming from. "I'm sorry?"

I plead with my friend for forgiveness. Whatever I have done, I want to take back. I stand up and walk toward him. I want to give him a hug. I stand in front of him, and for the first time notice the hand mark around the base of his throat. The bruising is deep and defined, leaving no question he has been strangled. I put my hand to his throat to lightly touch the deep bruise.

"Daniel, this is serious. This looks like a very real threat to your life. Please tell me who did this. Can we go to the police? We need to report this."

"Report this? What is this we need to report? You have no idea." He spits his words at me.

"I am sorry, please help me understand. I didn't mean to downplay any of this. I just think we need to talk to Sergeant Thomas. Let me call him for you."

"Don't you dare tell anyone! Anyone! You understand?"

"But Daniel, this is a crime. We need to report it."

"Are you daft? Police don't want to know about a tiff between two gays. They don't have the first clue how to respond to it. "Which one of you is the woman? They will ask. Or, why don't you guys just kiss and make up? They won't take this seriously. They don't know how, and the laws aren't there to protect people like me."

"People like you? Daniel, do you hear what you are saying? You can't excuse this because it was an act between two men. This is wrong. This is assault, no matter who is the victim and the perpetrator."

"Samara, just leave it alone. You have no idea what is going on here, and if you interfere, you will just make it worse."

I am shocked not only by the words I am hearing, but by the notion that somehow this isn't a singular event. The risk of this abuse escalating makes it even more of a priority to get some assistance from police, but my pleas to Daniel are falling on deaf ears. Daniel is certain he does not want to discuss this with anyone.

"I don't know what to say." I feel helpless, unable to know what more to do for my dear friend.

"Well, don't we know that!" he hisses.

There is a very real hatred in his voice as he scolds me. "Daniel, I don't know what this has to do with me." And then I stop, mid thought, as the possibilities come racing to my consciousness. "Oh my God Daniel, please tell me this wasn't my stalker? Did Robert do this to you?"

And it suddenly all becomes real - the strangulation a favourite attack of my ex-husband. I cringe at the memory of his dark eyes searing into mine as he holds me against my car, his hand tightening as he pins me against the hard, hot metal surface, restricting my oxygen intake just enough to allow me to feel dizzy. His words of promise for the ending of my life barely registering as he watches my eyes start to fall to the back of my head, and then he releases, and I drop to the ground, immediately reaching for the tender spot where his hand once was. Trying to massage the throat beneath my skin allowing the flow of air to pulse once more through the now injured vessels.

I bring my mind back to the present, back to the space I share with Daniel. I want to know more but I fear I really know the answer. Daniel has turned his back to me. He has his hand on his throat, gently holding his injury in his palm. He speaks slowly, but with a firm tone. "You should just go already. It will be better for everyone if you just leave."

I try to decipher the words I am hearing. They make no sense to me. I have never heard Daniel suggest such things before. I want to hold him. I want to make everything OK between us again, but his back is turned. He doesn't want to look at me.

I step toward him and place my palm on his upper arm. "I am sorry Daniel, for whatever I have done to upset you. Please forgive me. Let me help you."

"Help me?" he scoffs. "You can't even help yourself. Stop being so fucking righteous all of a sudden. As if you can do anything about this." He stops, fortunately, for with every word the anger is rising in him. The bitterness in tone cuts through me. "Stop making this about you. This has nothing to do with you!"

He pulls his arm away from me and takes a few steps forward, still not looking at me, his head bowed in silence.

"Please Daniel, let me help you," I beg. There are no more words I can say. I feel defeated. I am losing the argument here, and I don't know what to do.

"Just go!" he says sternly. He pauses, thinking carefully about his next words. "Just move, just run, hide, do whatever stupid fucking thing you have been doing. Just leave us all alone."

The tears begin to stream down my face. There are no words. I run for the front door and reef it open. I stride out into the sunlight. I pick up my pace as I run down the driveway and into the street. The sobbing takes away the last of my breath and I stop. I bend forward and allow the tears to flow. I have no idea what has just happened. I have no clue what I did. I cry not only for me but also for Daniel.

I find the local pathway to the beach, wiping my tears on the back of my hand. Small traces of mascara make their black mark on my skin. I try to breathe as I take the few steps to the sand. As I remove my shoes, I lean down and take them in my hand. I walk with a newfound determination. The white sand is hot beneath the soles of my feet. I pause and reach for the button on my shorts. I undo it and drop the garment to the sand. My hand finds the bottom of my t-shirt and I lift it above my head. The tears are still flowing but more slowly now. My breathing steadies me.

I drop my t-shirt on the pile of material on the sand. I don't delay and stride into the water. The liquid quickly gives me a refreshing light touch to my skin. I go deeper and deeper allowing the strong waves to crash against my body until I am waist deep and I dive under the water. I hold my breath and grab at the ocean floor. I look skyward and see the white foam of the wave above me crash overhead.

I hold my breath just that second too long as I feel my chest catch. I look around trying to last just a moment or two longer beneath the surface of the healing waters. The next wave is coming and I let go of the ocean floor to swim through the current that pulls to shore. I surface and I exhale the last of my breath. Instantly I gasp for air to fill my lungs once more. I dive again and am exhilarated by the pull of the strong sea. Over and over again I surface and dive. I do this for I know no other way to calm. Today, the ocean, even she cannot heal me.

TWENTY-ONE

Sitting at my desk later that day and staring at the white screen in front of me, I cannot write, for I cannot find the words to share anyone's story right now. All I can see, as my eyes glaze over looking at my laptop in front of me is Daniel - his face, his bruised, battered face and that mark around his neck. I can imagine the fear he must have felt as this man's hands squeezed down on his throat and close my eyes at the memories being triggered in my subconscious. If he felt even a tinge of the fear that I had known at the hands of my husband, it is too much to bear.

I look to my phone, my constant companion now as I check and re check for a return message from Daniel. I need to apologise to my friend. I pour my heart out via text and wait patiently for his response. But it is not forthcoming. I wonder when I should visit again. Leaving it a day or two seems sensible but I can't ignore the real medical danger Daniel is in at the moment. There have been countless stories of women told throughout the years, none more frightening than the woman who died a whole seventy-two hours after an attempted strangulation.

The bruising around the base of her neck came quickly and she had the good fortune and strength to seek safe refuge from her violent husband. Away from harm, she rested but the blood clots that had already formed through that one quick act killed her days after the terrifying experience first took place. I want to be there with Daniel. I want to monitor his wellbeing. First and foremost, I want him to get medical treatment. A full check-up. I only saw the marks on his face and neck. I can't imagine the horrors the rest of his body would uncover. But I understand Daniel's predicament. The shame and guilt of feeling as if you have allowed this to happen at the hands of the person you are intimate with.

I can see why Daniel wouldn't go to a hospital. I am exactly the same, even giving up now on reporting to police at all. The authorities and agencies there to help have failed us horribly, so much so that there seems little point in telling anyone. His words are on replay in my mind. "Just leave us alone." Who is he referring to when he speaks of us? Is he referring to the small community he has become very much a part of? Is he speaking of Shirley, of Thomas, even of Samuel? Or is he referring to the man who hurt him, his partner? Although I must admit Daniel has never spoken in detail about a relationship with any one person. I had imagined if he had started seeing someone he would have at least mentioned him in passing. Daniel is a complicated web of secrets and fake bravado. This is obvious to me now.

* * *

My lazy afternoon stretches out in front of me as I watch the beginnings of a tropical storm gather across the hinterland range. The peaks of the mountain disappear behind a shroud of white mist. A heavy rain is approaching. The clapping of thunder in the distance becomes louder with each march forward toward me. A flicker of lightning the constant companion for each sharp crack of thunder. A police-officer once told me that crooks, as he liked to call them don't do break and enters in the rain because they don't like to get wet. He laughed as he said it. A theory formed with years of call outs to unsuspecting victims of burglary.

This random statement has always given me a sense of safety in a storm, although I suspect for my stalker the opposite could very well be true. A heavy storm could provide the perfect cover for a murder. The screams not heard by anyone over the constant clamber of thunder. A heavy rain could prove the perfect remedy, for potentially washing away vital clues. Blood stains diluted and removed during the downpour. A murder weapon could be thrown into the choppy sea or cloudy waterway. Few people out in the weather to witness the strange comings and goings of a murder as it took place.

A cool breeze touches my skin. I close my laptop, find a soft blanket, pour myself a cold glass of wine and sit down on my deck to watch nature's light show spectacular. Part of me feels a little lonely - the perfect setting for a romantic interlude shared with no one. I wonder for a moment what Samuel is up to, and briefly ponder inviting him over, but I know he is busy. Besides I will see him soon enough. My fatigue overwhelms me and I close my eyes for a brief rest.

* * *

I feel warm. The heavy weight on my chest pushes down, and forces my laboured breath to wake me from my slumber. I open my eyes, and see his dark eyes staring back at me. In that second, his mouth closes in on mine. His tongue pushes past my lips, and searches my mouth frantically. He doesn't say a word. My ex-husband just takes what he believes is rightfully his. I push his torso with both palms, but his weight on top of me keeps him in place.

I struggle to move my mouth from Robert's, but he takes his hands and holds my head still. He is forceful and overpowering, yet not enough to cause me pain. I feel my breath responding to the panic, drawing my chest in and out in an attempt to survive. I fight back the tears welling in my eyes, helpless in this moment. My mind races with a million thoughts forming all at once, not one of them clear enough to aid my cause.

I try to murmur words but my mouth is unable to make the small movements to create the sounds. I am unsure whether to struggle, or resign to the fate that was destined to me years before. My ex-husband has tonight decided to carry out his murderous intent. He has found me asleep and vulnerable, alone and without defense. He has been watching, for years following me around the globe, and finally, today is the day he will seek his revenge.

My body weakens under the pressure of Robert's weight. My strength wavers now as it is beyond those few instant seconds when the rush of adrenalin floods the body with unimaginable capacity to fight or flee. That time has passed quickly, and I allow my mind to wander - to leave the body it failed to protect. I begin to think of seconds rather than hours for that is all I fear I will have left.

His mouth leaves mine, and his dark eyes search my face. He is looking at me in a way he hasn't been able to look at me for years. A sly smile encapsulates his face. He is pleased with himself. "Good evening, my wife." He utters the words that make my skin come alive.

"I am not your wife!" I say the words with the faint recognition that they may not actually be true.

"Oh Samara, of course you are. You will always be my wife." He smiles and his mouth touches mine once more. He kisses me quickly and resumes staring at me waiting for my reaction. I want to scream out. I want to cry. I can't believe that the legal proceedings to dissolve our marriage were delayed once more but this is exactly what I am hearing. The anger in me that had just moments earlier resolved itself to death, now reappears, to bubble from the depth of my stomach. Spreading like electricity through my nervous system reaching my limbs within seconds, the bolt of energy bursts through my hands.

I reach out, and slap him with the ferocity of years of pent up frustration. He looks stunned for just a moment before the realisation of my action dawns on him. He then throws his head back and laughs an evil soul-wrenching laugh that comes from a place of pure arrogance. He fears me not, for he has nothing but control over the situation, and he is not concerned with a petty slap from a woman.

His contorted face is the expression of elation at the response he is able to elicit from me. I am seething with unexplainable fury at his contempt, and react instinctively, reaching out to slap him once more. He responds quickly and grabs my palm just as it makes contact with his skin. My fingers are bent in his palm, and with the swift motion of his entrapment, my fingernails accidently dig deep into the flesh of his tanned cheek.

He lets my hand go immediately, and brings his palm to tend to the now fresh scratch marks on his skin. He feels the sticky hot moisture of his blood on his fingers, and stares down at his palm assessing the deep red colour of his own blood. His face reddens, and I realise my mistake. The fear rises in me as I recognise his expression switch once more to rage – a look I know too well.

"I am sorry," I beg him. "I didn't mean to scratch you." I silently pray he will show some understanding of my action. I would do anything right now to take back the few seconds that have just played out between us. "I honestly didn't mean to do that to you." I hardly know what more to say. I suspect no words will undo the damage I have done. In all the years of our marriage, I never once fought back. I never once marked or maimed him. That was his legacy for me alone.

My pleading goes unanswered as he is mesmerised by the betrayal that results in his own blood on his hands. He stares, obviously angered by the consequences of the one single act. "You marked me." He hisses at me.

"Please, please forgive me. I did not mean to hurt you." I beg him.

He throws his head back once more and laughs at me. "As if you could ever hurt me!"

"Please, don't hit me!" I beg, for I know what is coming next.

"It seems as if my wife has forgotten her place in the world." He says with complete control in his voice. He is beyond furious, and we both know how this game now plays out. "It seems you need a reminder of how to behave."

He raises his hand, and clenches his fingers together in a slow exaggerated movement. All to the delight of ensuring my agony is extended. A moment later, I feel the searing pain as his fist collides with my face. It feels as if every blood vessel in my brain simultaneously explodes at the same time as the darkness envelopes me. I lose consciousness slowly. My eyes lose focus. The last image I see is my ex-husband standing over me.

I am no longer able to fight back in any way. This is the end. I will not wake from this.

TWENTY-TWO

An enormous clap of thunder rings through my ears. My skin is sensitive to the cold wind blowing on my soaking wet body. I hear another noise. When I come to, there are muffled sounds and warm hands on me. My eyes flutter open, my focus not yet returned as I slowly try to turn my head. A sharp pain tears my head back to its original position.

"Stay still," the voice instructs me. "An ambulance is on its way." The voice sounds friendly.

I want to stand. I place my hands on the hard deck below me. The wind blows and the rain streams down on my face. I am beyond cold. My body is registering a shiver that resonates through to my bones. For the first time, I sense the sweet taste of blood in my mouth. I let my tongue explore the split in my bottom lip, and I retract it quickly. The pain at the touch to the injury is too intense for me to manage.

My vision has not yet returned. The image before me is blurry, with only the voice giving me a clue as to its identity. "Daniel?" I ask, hopeful it is indeed my friend sitting beside me now.

"Just stay still. I think you have a concussion. I couldn't wake you." The words make sense now. I am alive. I am in pain through my entire body. I am unsure if I can move my back at all to sit up, but I am comforted that I am not alone. I try to shield my eyes from the pelting rain as it intensifies but my arm is too weak to move much beyond the hard surface beneath me.

"Don't move. Please…please. Stay still," Daniel begs of me. He looks around and seeing what he is searching for and stands up. I hear the scraping noise of metal on wood drawing closer to me. Daniel pulls the table to me and lifts the two metal legs over my body. The flat glass surface of the tabletop acts as a shield against the extreme weather. Daniel crawls partially under the table and for the first time I can open my eyes to see him more clearly.

A clap of thunder makes him jump. "We are probably going to get electrocuted under here you know." He smiles a little to try to bring humour to the dire situation. I look up at him focusing on his still swollen face. He looks as bad as I feel. And then I remember him - my stalker, Robert, my ex-husband, still probably somewhere nearby. He is most likely still in the house.

"Daniel. Be careful. Robert, he is here!" I string together a few incoherent words of warning to my friend.

"There is no one here, Samara." He pauses. "I came over to say sorry. When you didn't answer, I came up through the back stairs and found you here all alone."

"No, Daniel! He is here. He hit me! I can't remember after that. But he might still be inside the house. Be careful Daniel please."

"Shh, Samara. Don't worry about that now. Just relax and wait for the ambulance. I am going to go and open the front door for them. Just stay still, OK?"

He waits for me to say yes and he stands up. I hear his footsteps walk slowly into the house, and I wait anxiously for his safe return. I begin putting the pieces of my last memory together. Robert, here on the deck with me, his strong body on top of mine as it held me in place. I remember thinking I was about to die. Feeling hot, the heat of anger rising in my body and then the slap. The moment that sealed my fate or so I had thought. Why am I still alive? Why did he not kill me when he had the perfect chance to do so?

The rain eases for a moment but the wind blows through the deck. I notice again the cold of the rain soaked through my clothes. I wonder how long I have been lying here. It is dark still. It is nighttime, hopefully of the same day. What day is it even? My mind is still foggy as I struggle to place myself in exactly the right day, month and year. My head throbs in pain. I try in vain to raise my arm to ensure the top of my head is still in place. Where is Daniel? What is taking him so long?

I try to call out his name and manage nothing more than a whisper. My throat although soaking wet on the outside is dry and abrasive on the inside. I hear footsteps, multiple footsteps - they are taking their time. An unknown person stops beside me. He bends down to reveal a concerned expression. His clean white shirt is dry underneath a red waterproof jacket. His body is partially under the table as he shines a small torch into one eye and then the next. "Can you tell me your name?" he asks me.

I think for a minute and nod slightly. "Samara Sanders." I say softly so as not to irritate my throat.

"Yes, that's right," he assures me. The paramedic is professional and sensitive to my delicate situation. "Do you feel any pain anywhere?"

I think for a minute before answering, doing a quick physical assessment of my body. "My neck...my head...my throat...my arm...my lip." I let my tongue touch it again to confirm the pain emulating from my bloodied lip. "Everywhere hurts, I think."

He retrieves something from his bag and I watch as he places the green object in my line of vision. "Here, I will put this in your mouth. Inhale, as you need to. It will give you some relief. We have to stretcher you from here, so I want you to try to remain still. This may take a few moments." I listen to the instructions and will myself to obey.

I want to thank him, but I am beginning to feel nauseous from the pain. As I gratefully accept the green whistle, I take a hesitant mouthful of the relief promised inside.

"Daniel? Where is he?" I feel the sudden need to ensure my friend's wellbeing. He didn't return from opening the front door to the paramedics and I wonder what he might be doing.

"Your friend said he couldn't stay," the kind medic informs me. "Look, it is none of my business, but whatever went on here..." He stops, having some advice to give but hesitant in offering it. "Look, I'm just saying I attend too many overdoses, and you and your friend should think about getting some help."

"What?" I am confused as to the illicit drug reference, if that is what he is indeed hinting at.

"Your friend begged me not to notify police, which I assured him I wasn't obliged to do in this case. He cleared the lines away, but this is obviously a problem for both of you."

I try to shake my head. I squint my eyes as if the mere action of doing so will force all this new information to make sense. "I don't understand. I didn't take anything. I don't use drugs." I try to sound confident, and with every right to be, as I know I didn't consume anything other than a glass of wine prior to falling asleep on my deck in the rain.

"You have obviously had a bad fall. We won't know how bad it is until we get some tests done, but this has to be the wakeup call for you to stop using drugs."

I am dumbfounded. I simply fail to understand why I am being lectured for something I did not do. Isn't it bad enough that I lay here on the deck barely able to move, with injuries the latest present from a vengeful ex-husband intent on punishing me? Why must I now listen to this sanctimonious lecture from someone who has not even the first clue of what I do? I look at my rescuer and want to say more, but don't have the strength. He must see the frustration welling up in me.

"Enough said. Lecture over. Your friend has removed the substances, which is good enough for me. I am not involving police here. I hardly think you two are running the streets trying to sell the stuff. I just hope you find a more suitable alternative to relaxing nights at home. Just think about it."

He has said enough, and continues to administer his first aid, applying a neck brace before having his partner assist with the stretcher. I take another dose of the pain relief, for the first didn't seem to quite cover the extent of the damage to my body.

* * *

As I sit up in hospital later the next day, having heard from the doctors and been given the all clear of any serious head injury, I am thankful that things weren't worse. I felt certain that my stalker would kill me, and my mind continues to try to process why he didn't. He had the perfect chance to murder me without witnesses and make a quick clean exit from the scene. Yet he failed to complete the task of which I have been certain he is determined to finish.

"Oh darling, don't be silly." I hear the exaggerated consonants of Daniel's flippant tone in the hallway outside of my room. I sincerely hope he is here to see me. He turns the corner and enters my room like the rock star he imagines he is. He gasps at the sight of me. "Oh my!" he hollers as he raises one hand to his chest. "What have you done to yourself?" He wastes no time in presenting me with the mirror that I had so far avoided.

"Is it that bad?" I cringe, hoping that Daniel is just being Daniel and being over dramatic in his criticism of my facial injuries.

"Oh, darling. I hope you weren't planning on getting laid again this year, because in all truth, you hold little hope of any man coming near you with a face like that!" He raises his hand over his mouth, mocking me all the while.

"Is it really that bad?"

"Well, my sweet, it is hard to tell where your top lip finishes and your nose starts. Oh, who cares really? You are still a sexy minx."

I notice for the first time that not only is Daniel in high spirits, but his own facial swelling and bruising has all but vanished. "How is it possible that you are nearly fully recovered?" I ask him.

"Good genes, my darling. I recover quickly, just like my dear old mother." He leans over the bed to whisper the rest of the statement to me. "Oh, and this little bottle of magic potion I found that clears bruising. Quite handy, I might add, for those extra special moments with an especially exuberant lover."

I dare not ask more. I certainly do not need any further information about Daniel's love life than I already have embedded in my memory banks. I do, though, want more information about what

Daniel might have seen the night before. "Daniel, how did you find me last night?"

"Just where you were, laying on the floor in the rain, unconscious. You gave me quite the fright. I didn't think I could wake you, so I called the paramedics."

"Did you see anyone else there? Was anyone in the house? Did you see any cars or anyone leaving when you arrived?"

"Nope, nothing. You were all alone my darling. Like the solitary little single girl, you are. Quite sad, really."

I ignore Daniel's jibe remark at my single life. A little rude, really, considering he himself isn't partnered up and living out the white picket fence dream of happily ever after.

"And the paramedic said that there were lines of cocaine in the house. And that you removed it?"

"Yes, I did. But fear not, it did not go to waste. A little party last night took care of the last of that stash. Nice stuff, by the way. Where did you get that little party favour from?"

"Daniel, I didn't. You know I don't do cocaine." I was certain I didn't do the lines, and I was currently struggling to understand how it could be in my house. "Had you left some there from when you were staying over perhaps?"

"Oh dear, I may be extravagant, but I'm not about to leave perfectly good lines of cocaine laying around." He chuckles to himself at the mere suggestion of it.

"I don't understand any of this." I beg for some simple explanation from him.

"You haven't understood a lot of what has supposedly been happening to you lately. The writing on the mirror, the sand heart in the car, not one but two mobile phones not working, the damage to your tyre. Now, you present this confession that you don't remember having cocaine in your house. Do you think maybe you need to see someone?"

I gasp at the suggestion and the realisation that my friend no longer believes that I have a stalker following me and messing with my mind. "Daniel, you don't believe me?"

"It's not that I don't believe you. There is an element of truth in every work of fiction. We are writers, my dear, and sometimes the storyline gets muddled in our head with our reality. Bound to happen, even to the best of us." He stops, and ponders the thought for a moment longer. "Well, not to me, my dear, of course. But it could certainly happen to you. This is your first fiction work of a genre outside of romance, isn't it?"

"Yes, but I hardly understand how this could explain everything that has happened in this last week or so. Or for the last few years, I might add."

"Yes, yes, my little one. Of course." He stops himself short of saying any more.

"No, don't do that!" I raise my voice a little, feeling the need to be taken seriously for a change, and not knowing any other way of doing so.

"Do what?" Daniel raises his hand to his chest once more. "What could you possibly be accusing me of?"

"Don't dismiss my feelings so quickly. I know what is happening here. I don't expect you to understand, but I don't appreciate you just explaining it away with a judgmental reference to my mental health."

"Oh dear, I didn't mention your mental health. You did that all by yourself."

"See…that! You throw those words around like they aren't going to hurt my feelings, but they do. Sometimes, Daniel, you are so flippant with other people's emotions."

"Oh, my silly girl, that is because I don't deal in emotions. They are a useless waste of my time."

I shake my head. There really is no reasoning with that logic. And my friend is correct. He really doesn't have the time or capacity to deal with such wasteful endeavours as the expression of emotions. Besides lust, maybe, if that is even considered an emotion.

I suddenly remember the important question I need to ask of Daniel. "Where is Samuel? Did you contact him?"

"Yes, of course I called your little cowboy the minute I left the house." He remembers something important. "Oh, and here is your phone by the way." He produces my mobile from his pocket. I had wondered where my phone was, and had assumed, that, my stalker must have taken it with him.

Daniel's response doesn't quite provide the explanation I was hoping for. "So, did Samuel want to see me?"

"See you?" He laughs, his head thrown back in a dramatic fashion. "I am sure that poor little cowboy has seen just about enough of you to last him a lifetime. He was here all night. Don't you remember? He was thrown out early this morning by the staff when they needed to send you for more x-rays. Don't you remember him sitting in that chair through the night?"

I turn to the leather recliner set against the wall of the small room. "He stayed here?"

"Yes, of course your little boyfriend was here. He let me know he had to go, but said he would be back to take you home as soon as you were able to be released."

I smile at the thought of my beautiful Samuel staying with me through the night.

"Oh, stop with that lovely crap already. I am sick to death of seeing it." Daniel pauses. "I hope it has registered with you that you are not exactly sexy temptress material at the moment. If I were him, you wouldn't have had a second chance with me. You better try harder, my dear, if you want to keep that prime piece of meat interested."

TWENTY-THREE

I can't wait to be released from hospital. Forty-eight hours imprisoned against my will for the sake of observation is more than I can manage. But I did it, remaining as patient as I could with the endless questions to assess my capacity for memory. The constant indirect references to my mental health and alleged drug use wore away at me. I could not wait to throw on the clothes Daniel had reluctantly collected from my house for me to escape through the hospital doors.

Spending time with Samuel inside the hospital room was not how I wanted our relationship to start. I was thankful for the time he spent with me, and felt extremely grateful that he wanted to be by my side for much of my entrapment. I was excited about getting out, and continuing to get to know my new lover better in the real world.

In the end, it was Daniel who won out the battle to take me home, suggesting to Samuel that he had already monopolised more than enough of my time. In the car on the way home, Daniel was once more in fine form. "So what now, sugar cakes? Want to go home and get fucked up?"

"I hardly think so. I am going home to crawl into my own bed with a book and a cup of tea."

"A cup of tea?" Daniel injects in his best British accent, whilst pointing his pinky in the air in the mime of sipping tea.

"Yes. Tea and bed… and in that order."

"Alone again I presume?" Daniel doesn't pause for a moment for me to recover from my injuries before reminding me yet again that I am planning a quiet night at home. Samuel was of course keen to be by my side but I felt as if I needed some alone time and rest for the night.

"Yes alone, of course. You said yourself. I am not in any state to be entertaining company at the moment. I don't want to see Samuel again until the swelling and redness dissipate a little more. I have hardly known him long enough to expect him to sit through this ugliness any longer than he has already and still want to shag me."

"Oh, tea and shagging. How very English and conservative of you, my darling." Daniel laughs at me one more. "So, when are you seeing that hot little piece of actor again?"

If only Daniel knew the truth. It was pure torture keeping Samuel at bay. As soon as he found out I was in hospital, he rushed straight up to be by my side. But I could not fully explain how the injuries happened to me and I know he is going to ask for more details. I don't know quite how to explain to him what exactly happened to me. It is all so very overwhelming for me, and I haven't known Samuel long enough for him to not assume like everyone else that I am losing my mind.

"Hello?" Daniel is keen to get into the juicy details of my love life with me. "So, when?"

"I'm thinking just another day or two and most of the swelling will have gone down."

"What did you tell him happened?" Daniel asks me, hesitantly.
"I said I fell."

Daniel turns to me, mouth gaping open. "So, you do now believe that you imagined it all?"

"No!" I give a firm response. It just seems that people are unable or unwilling to hear the truth and I don't know how much to tell Samuel about what everyone else seems to fail to want to acknowledge as fact.

Daniel lets out a weighty sigh. "Oh, sweetness. You know I love you, don't you?" He says in his best parent voice. He waits for my response before continuing.

"Yes, I guess." I finally decide to agree, for without consent I know he will not continue this statement.

"Well, I do, of course, sweet cheeks. But you have to understand how we all feel. Not one other person has seen this so-called stalker but you. Not Shirley when she picked you up on the side of the road. Not me when I supposedly walked in just after your attack. Not the police…"

I interject. "The police aren't even trying to look for him."

"And what does that tell you sweetie?" He pauses, waiting again for my compliance in the form of an answer.

"I don't know. Why don't you go ahead and tell me?" I feel the frustration in me rising.

"It says that they think he isn't real. That you are going a little crazy darling, and they haven't the time or the inclination to chase after a figment of your imagination."

The words are cutting. Daniel once more says it exactly how he sees it. I know he is correct. The police, the paramedic, the doctors at the hospital - not a single one seemed to even entertain my story that my stalker had hit me and knocked me to the ground. Instead, they choose to believe that I was high and stoned or drunk, and simply fell and hit my head. No drug tests were given, no evidence collected. Police this time were not even called to ask their investigative questions of me.

The drive home resolved no further questions for either of us. Daniel made a vague mention of a certain man he was planning on seeing later that night for sex and drinks, as he called it. I couldn't wait to just get home, have a shower and slip into something comfortable. After my shower, I planned on grabbing a book from my endless reading list, making a hot tea and crawling into bed.

I didn't plan on sleeping but my body was still so stiff and sore that bed seemed the only comfortable option for me at the moment. Once home I throw on an oversized t-shirt and indulge in a few pieces of chocolate to accompany the tea. I feel like an elderly resident in a nursing home, crawling into bed while the sun is still in the sky.

I read chapter after chapter but it isn't long before my eyes grow tired and my body stiff from the semi-upright position on the bed. I close my book and rest my eyes. As sleep finds me, my last conscious thoughts are of him. I think grimly of Robert, my stalker who is never far away and visiting frequently these days. I imagine it is not long before I see him again. This time though, I plan to be ready for him.

A body slumps on my bed beside me. He is the weight and height of a grown man, about six-foot-tall and ninety kilograms, if I was to estimate. He is approximately the same statistics as my stalker. I awake with a fright, ready to fight to the death. I lash out and throw the first punch into mid-air. My eyes are still focusing on the bright room around me, unsure exactly where to aim the hard-hitting attack.

"Oh!" My surprise guest screeches out into the open room. "Why did you do that?" He demands to know.

"Daniel?" I recognise the voice and soon after the face. "What are you doing here?"

"Oh, my darling Samara, did you forget again? I am here for lunch as we arranged. Seriously girl, this forgetfulness of yours is getting boring already."

"What? Lunch? I had lunch at the hospital before you drove me home remember."

"Samara, that was yesterday." Daniel sighs obviously frustrated with my lack of a concept of reality.

"Have I slept for a whole day?" I ask him.

"Have you not even got out of bed since you got home?" Daniel seems disgusted by the thought.

"No, I don't think so. The last thing I did was make a tea and crawl into bed with a book." I look beside me and the empty teacup is on the bedside table. My phone empty of all charge sits beside it. It would appear I have slept for an entire twenty-four hours.

"Well, hurry up and get your skanky ass out of bed and shower. Please shower. And a little foundation wouldn't hurt. I don't need to be looking at that face while I am trying to eat if you don't mind."

As always Daniel takes my mind off my major worries and helps me focus on what is important in life - food and an appropriate beauty regime.

"And I think we should get back to writing today. So I have brought some goodies with me." He lifts a small transparent bag full of his favourite white substance and dangles it in front of my face. "I have also brought food with me, from your favourite little vegan place, God help me that I ever have to walk into that hippie heaven again, and today's cocktail is an old favourite of mine, the cock sucking cowboy."

"No!" I shout back at him. "No cocktails! Especially not shots."

"Whatever white girl!" He throws the comment over his shoulder as he exits my room.

"You are white too Daniel!" This man is exhausting and at the same time I relish his company far too much.

I relinquish on the cocktails and allow Daniel to make me one of his infamous espresso martinis. It is after all like breakfast for me after such a long sleep and a coffee inspired cocktail seems to be a good compromise. The food is delicious and I devour mine in minutes. The nourishment gives me a fresh bout of energy that I haven't felt in days.

"So..." Daniel begins. And I know that something big is coming. He is rarely reluctant to speak his mind and I can't even guess at what is behind his current thinking. "So, where to next for you?" he enquires.

I feel a little taken back by the question. "Daniel, are you tired of me already?" I hope this isn't the case, but need to ask the question of him.

"Not quite yet, but getting there." He turns to me, and smiles, as he engulfs me in a giant hug to let me know his humour is with good intent. "I was just wondering what country you might run to next."

"Well if I tell you that, it wouldn't be a secret hideaway then would it?" I humour him.

"Well, if you don't trust me. That's fine!" He explodes immediately as he drops his arms from around me.

"Stop Daniel. Stop!" I am quick to douse the flames of his volatile self-esteem. "I'm just joking with you. What makes you ask that question anyway? Do you think I should leave already?"

"No." He responds quickly. "I am not completely finished with you yet."

I am relieved to hear. "So, why ask?" I am curious as to why this question has come up all of a sudden.

"Well, I just assume that you would be ready to leave soon considering the latest incident." Daniel chooses that word carefully. "And besides, I thought I could use a little bit of a holiday."

I am surprised at his suggestion and for once happy to admit that I was wrong about Daniel's line of questioning. He has raised a great idea. He wants to join me for part of my next big adventure.

"Really?" As soon as the question leaves my mouth, I know I haven't quite got the tone right. "What I mean to say is…I would love for you to join me!"

I have been quietly contemplating my next place of residence. I always seem to let my mind wander to what next. Partly I imagine it is for security reasons but also partly so as not to get too connected to any one place. Staying alive and that means staying moving is the most crucial part of my survival plan.

"How about Hawaii?" I suggest the destination that had in my quiet planning been rising quickly to the top of the list as the next preferred home for a little while.

Daniel thinks for a minute. "The sun has been playing havoc with my skin here. How about a colder climate?"

I do a mental run through of the cities in my head. "How about Berlin? Is that cold enough for you?"

"Brilliant!" He exclaims. When do we leave?

I am surprised but overjoyed with the prospect that my next venture might not be a solo trip. I have so many questions to ask of Daniel including how long he might stay with me in Berlin but for some reason one question is more pressing than the rest. "Daniel, what about this mystery man you've been seeing?"

"What? What man?" He seems genuinely surprised at the question.

"You seem to always be rushing off to see someone. To meet some mystery man who is picking you up. You won't tell be anything about who you have been seeing, so I guessed it was something more than just a random hook up."

"Don't be a drama queen. I am not seeing anyone. I simply do not have time for such meaningless pursuits as a relationship my dear. Who has time for that rubbish?"

"Ok, so Berlin it is!"

"But what about dear old Samuel? How are you going to explain you running away to Europe to him?" Daniel makes a good point and one that I haven't fully explored yet. I really feel something for Samuel already and I don't know how to explain to him that I am suddenly about to leave.

TWENTY-FOUR

Days pass before I feel ready to meet Samuel again. As suggested by my date, we plan to finally have the dinner that we missed out on. Samuel kindly offers to pick me up from my house and this time I don't resist. Not after the last disaster. This time I want nothing to go wrong. There is so much to try to explain to him. I only hope he understands and wants to continue to see me for the brief time that I have left in this little piece of paradise.

Exactly on schedule, Samuel arrives and I skip to the car to meet him before he has time to arrive at my front door. I am keen to spend some time away from the house after being shut in for days now. I am also certain that my stalker is never far away and I don't need to let him see Samuel.

I jump in the car, and smile as soon as I see him. The electricity between us is undeniable, even though I have never felt less desirable in my entire life. "You look beautiful," Samuel is quick to reassure me.

"Thank you." I reach over to kiss him, for not doing so would crush my soul. I am mere inches from his lips when that current rushes through his skin to mine, and I feel alive. Our lips touch, as he reaches in and pulls me tighter. His hands fumbling with excitement,

I can feel this insane reaction in him too. No man has ever made me feel the way Samuel does when our bodies are close.

For a moment, I toy with the idea of skipping dinner altogether, of walking back into the house, of retiring to my bedroom, and staying put for days with Samuel. I desire nothing more than to be with him - to enjoy every last second, we have together. I strengthen my resolve, and release his mouth from mine. I stare into his gorgeous blue eyes, and smile a smile of pure happiness. I feel safe for just an instant - safe in this car with the man whom I know would protect me from anything. I wish I could share my deepest darkest secrets with him, but there isn't time. I have already started my planning for my next big move.

Samuel moves his hands to the wheel gripping tightly, I can sense that he too would have liked to take the kiss further. "OK, so should we make a start for the restaurant?" I sense that he is testing me, to see if I indeed want to move this date straight to the bedroom. I pause for a moment, and ponder my options and feel my stomach sound with hunger. Dinner is definitely in order. A nightcap can wait for later.

As Samuel pulls the car out slowly into the street, I feel a sense of relief being in his company again. It has been days since I have seen my stalker, which has left me wondering when he will reappear again. At least for now, in the car with Samuel, I am assured that my stalker can't reach me. The drive to the restaurant isn't far, and we take the short cut that became the road I will forever remember as the place I met my ex-husband once more. I try not to think about that night as we pass the exact location where my car stopped. My wheel deflated to the point that the sound of scraping metal on the bitumen sang its sure demise.

I turn to Samuel who is quiet - deep in thought, or so it would appear. Something catches his eye, and I look into the distance before us to see the flashing red and blue lights of the fire truck. It's siren not yet required on this lonely stretch of road, but its speed indicating an urgency that leaves me feeling uneasy. I look into Samuel's eyes. "It always makes me feel for the people who they are rushing to help."

"I know," Samuel agrees as he reaches over and takes my hand in his. He, like me, is an empath - a person in touch with the emotion and needs of others. It is a rare quality and a good match for the sensitive writer. "Let's hope everything is OK for the people they are going to help and that they get there in time."

I silently agree. I love this quality about Samuel - this amazing sense of care and humility. He is so unlike what I imagined a successful actor to be. The sensationalism the media heralds about the film industry gives the general public entirely the wrong perception from what I have gathered from my limited experience.

Arriving at the restaurant, we wait for a moment to be seated as Samuel looks at his phone. His expression changes as he looks at the messages on the screen in front of him. He turns toward me, a worried look overwhelming his gorgeous face.

"Samara, I have to go!" His voice is monotone. He doesn't explain more. He doesn't need to. I can see it is serious.

"Can I come with you?" I ask, not wanting to leave him alone for whatever has struck him down.

"Yes." He turns and begins to run to the car. I am just a step behind.

He takes to the wheel. The peaceful drive of moments earlier is replaced by a reckless speed as the car weaves in and out of the nighttime traffic in the town centre. It isn't long before we are cleared of the obstruction, and we are headed to the beachside location that houses both of our residences. I don't know quite what to make of what is transpiring, and I can see Samuel is concentrating, so I don't intrude on his thoughts. I am sure that at the pace we are covering the distance between the restaurant and our final destination, it won't be long before all becomes clear.

I place my hand on Samuel's leg, just to let him know that I am near. The car quickens once more as I recognise our surrounds. We are mere blocks from Samuel's house, and for the first time I look skyward and see it - the black smoke beckoning us, swirling and spiralling into the night air. The bright orange and gold flames dancing beneath the clear horizon, as if their sole purpose is to send the smoky signal skywards.

I cover my mouth to restrain the gasp as the pieces come together, the speeding fire engine; the message on his phone; the smoke in the distance. I fear we are about to find Samuel's house alight. I involuntarily squeeze Samuel's leg a little tighter. He must finally feel my presence as he turns to me. "Max!" He says the name of his trusted companion out loud; his most urgent thought is of his much-loved dog.

The tears quickly fill my eyes. I cannot imagine the anguish going through his heart right now. I close my eyes for a second and say a silent prayer for Max in the hope that we find him alive and well.

The car pulls up as close to the house as emergency crews will allow us. Samuel jumps out immediately, and runs to the front line of emergency workers, stopping only as he is caught by one and restrained from moving closer. I stand back and search the gathering crowd, fearing I might recognise a certain face.

The heat from the fire reaches my skin and I walk around the crowd to search for some shelter. I don't want to be far from Samuel, but I need to allow him to do whatever he has to do right now. I see what I guess are his concerned neighbours staring into the dancing flames as they engulf what is left of Samuel's house. I can see in their eyes the fear they have for their own homes if the fire is not contained. The fire crews, numerous in numbers are working to contain the spread, shouting instructions to each other as they go about the role they have trained expertly to complete.

The crowd is pushed further back from the heavy smoke and that is when I see him. Robert, brazen and unashamed, standing staring at the house as it and everything inside of it is destroyed. The fire started by his very own hands, I hold no doubt of that. All fear of this known danger escapes me as I march over to confront the madman. As I step closer, I see him, Max, Samuel's loyal dog on a leash sitting obediently beside my ex-husband. The lead is held tight, secured at one end to Max's collar. The other end held carefully in Robert's hand.

I stop for a minute as I try to process the confused imagery presented to me. This proves, without a doubt, that my ex-husband set the fire that is currently destroying my lover's home. But why would he save Samuel's dog? Why prove beyond a doubt that he is behind it by having Max on a lead, taken from the house and away from danger before the fire had time to spread?

I step forward again as my stalker senses my approach. He turns and grins a smirk that is caught in the reflection of the dancing flames, the moving light and shade producing an eerie graphic imagery to his murderous glare. I bound closer to him and begin to yell. "What have you done?"

He instantly grabs my hand and pulls me closer, holding me by the wrist. "Quiet now, or I won't let you have the little doggie back."

He is holding Max for ransom. He is making it known to me that he has spared the life of the dog. He has no fear of being caught. This is yet another attempt by a madman at total control and manipulation.

"What do you want?" I ask.

"You stop this affair with your lover boy there." He nods his head in the direction of my date for the night. He has stood in the crowd, watching with amusement as Samuel speaks to the emergency workers obviously frantic for news of his pet.

I look to Samuel, and then back again to my ex-husband. I put out my other hand to accept the lead from him. "I agree." I say without question. I would do anything now to save the life of my lover's beautiful bulldog.

I feel the tightness of his grip around my wrist ease, but know the pressure has been enough to surely leave another bruise. He speaks again, quietly as to not be overheard, but with a certainty that only a sociopath could manage. "Do you understand what you have just agreed to?"

"Yes," I say softly. The ache in my heart is immediate as I recognise the end to my time with Samuel has come far too early.

"You will not see him again. You will say no further words. You can hand him back his dog, but you explain nothing. You never see him again." Robert is making his demands crystal clear to me.

I stare directly into his eyes. All fear vanishes. His presence in this crowd is no threat to me. He knows I am waiting to take Max from him. He makes me stand and wonder about his next move as punishment for my self-confidence. The reality is that I truly have no idea what he is capable of doing next.

"I said I agree."

"Say, please." The words slither from his mouth.

"What?" I don't understand what he is asking of me now.

"Ask nicely, and say please." He pauses. "Say to me, please, my husband, can I have my friend's dog back?"

My chest tightens. He is toying with me. He is making me beg for the animal. He has complete control. I turn to look at Samuel for a minute, his face now scanning the crowd, searching for Max, or for me. I can't delay, and have Samuel find me and walk over to us.

I return my stare once more to my stalker, and say the words that he needs to hear from me. "Please, my husband, may I have my friend's dog back?"

He smiles. Obviously, pleased to have me in this position. He is relying on my willing participation to play his evil game.

"Give me a kiss on the lips to thank me for rescuing the dog."

I shake my head in disgust. I can't imagine the mind of this madman that he wants me to suffer in this way. My chest once more heaves at the thought of what I am about to do, but I don't dare delay any longer as time is of the essence right now. I learn forward and kiss the lips of the man who has just burned down the house in front of us. This is the man who has carefully planned and carried out the malicious damage to my lover's residence and to every last possession inside his home. Everything Samuel owned has gone up in flames, everything except for his much-loved pet that Robert now holds for ransom in his pursuit to torture me further.

I hold my breath the entire time my lips are on his, not wanting any more of the essence of me to be given away to this madman than what I am obliged to give. I keep my eyes closed, not wanting to look directly into the eyes of the man who will one day kill me. When I pull away, he has an evil smile sprayed across his face. His dark eyes register a smug sense of self-satisfaction - he has achieved what he came here tonight to do, proving once more that he is in control of my entire life, and ultimately, my death.

He places the end of Max's led into my palm, then turns to walk away. No further words need to be said. I glance back at the last place I saw Samuel, and he is staring back at me, his face the combined expression of surprise and despair. It is obvious he has seen the kiss. I begin to walk to him as he steps towards me. He sees me and looks down at Max, who is now overjoyed to be reunited with his owner.

Samuel pats the top of Max's head to contain his excitement. His eyes don't leave mine. "Who was that?"

I simply shake my head, for no words can explain what I need to say to Samuel. If he hasn't already worked it out, he will soon enough. I can't find a way to explain what has just happened, and I don't think I want to dare imagine what will happen next if I stay a moment longer. I can feel my stalker watching me, his presence hidden from view. Staring at us, watching and hoping that I will carry out his demand to end my affair with my new lover.

"I'm sorry." I utter the words as I turn to walk away. I don't want to see Samuel's face as he registers the hurt and betrayal that he will feel as I leave him. I pass the lead to Samuel, and run through the crowd pushing past the curious onlookers. Fortunately for both of us, Samuel doesn't follow.

I feel for my phone in my pocket and immediately I choose the number to dial. It rings just once before it is picked up.

"Daniel, can you please come and get me?" My voice is shaky as the emotion begins to spill over.

"Of course," Daniel agrees without delay. "Where are you?"

"I'm going to the point. Meet me there."

TWENTY-FIVE

I stand at the furthest edge of the high rocky cliff face, void of all emotions. The run from Samuel's house exhausting every last withering fragment of energy I have left in my body. I look down to the waves below as they crash against the large boulders that form this natural headland, wave after wave relentless in their pursuit smash against the rock face. The purpose and intent of the orchestrated movements of the ocean, as certain, as they have been for centuries.

The rhythm of the sea calms me as it always does. The wild waves entice me with their call. I look down, and imagine diving into the fierce waters below. The wind catches my dress and blows the material high above my waist. I grab the hem of the skirt, and with one movement, remove the flimsy material from my body. The ferocious wind catches the fabric and carries the dress into the night sky. I watch it flutter for a moment then finally fall into the dark ocean beneath me.

The salt air finds my skin, and licks the surface of my arms, my legs and my stomach. A fragment of stray hair catches in my open mouth, and I reach up and allow the long strands of red curls to be released from the tie that holds them in place.

The wind catches my hair and immediately my eyes are covered with a thick layer of the rich red strands. I briefly imagine the colour I should choose next, my natural blonde long ago discarded to hide my true identity. Chestnut, ash blonde, burgundy, grey, pink? I have no preference as to my next disguise. The mere thought of it weakens my resolve.

What if I stop? What if I stop running? Stop hiding? What if I stop it all right now?

The night air feels cold on my newly awakened soul. I look down once more at the sea beneath me calling for my entrance. The dark water and the white caps are clearly visible under the light of the moon even from the vast height of the cliff face. I sense them all so vividly now. I yearn to dive into the warm embrace of the mistress called the sea and feel her liquid energy heal me once more.

I close my eyes and breathe in her intoxicating aroma. I need to feel the warm waters on my skin, through my hair, covering every inch of me. I want to let the ocean heal my soul. I take a step. I can feel her call. She wants to take away my pain. I breathe her deep into my lungs. I imagine floating, then falling into her.

"Samara!" The panicked voice alerts me to his presence. "Samara, step back!" the voice yells again.

My foggy mind takes a moment to register my friend's command. I turn to see him. His face is clearly distressed as he runs to my spot on the edge of the cliff. The movement unbalances me, and I wobble. I raise my hands to steady myself, and look down at the sheer drop beneath me. It would be so easy to let myself fall.

"Samara!" Daniel yells again. "Stop!"

This one word sends an alarm to my brain, which switches it back to life. I take a step back to steady myself. Without it, a fall to my watery grave would be inevitable. Just as the sole of my foot connects with the ground behind me, Daniel is in front of me. He has his arms around me and he pushes me to the ground. His body pins me to the solid flooring of mother earth.

Daniel's breathing is heavy, and I feel myself inhale and exhale in time to him. The pain only now begins to register. The sensation of the hard rock beneath me as it digs into my spine and the slight trickle of a warm substance I recognise as my own blood spills a little from the small indentation to the back of my head. The wind howls around us, letting out an animalistic noise to register its discontent. A strong wave crashes against the rocks beneath us, and I imagine I feel the sea spray captured in the air. The sprinkle of the salty magic falling now on my face wakes me from my dreamlike state.

Daniel isn't speaking, his shock at finding me on the cliff face having rendered him without words. I am speechless. My mind barely processes what has just happened. The weight of Daniel's body lightens. His hand finds my wrist, that just moments earlier, was entrapped by my stalker. It is held firmly now by my friend. "Samara. We need to get out of here!" He talks to me as if I am a child. He looks at me approvingly waiting for any indication of my willingness to oblige to his request.

I nod in agreement. My mouth is dry, the words unable to find their way from my brain to my lips. Daniel stands up and drags me to my feet. With me in front of him, he manoeuvres us along the narrow pathway to the fence line. Once there, he lifts my legs and torso over the steel structure that is the boundary fence. I am, for the first time, aware of my modesty, as my G-string and lace bra does little to hide my curves.

Daniel doesn't let go of my wrist as he quickly mounts the rail in one manly leap. His athleticism impressive even to me, a writer whose only exercise is getting smashed in the waves. Once over the fence, Daniel lets out a massive sigh. Relief, I assume, that we are both out of immediate danger of falling.

"What are you doing? You were going to fall!" He explains his distress in more detail, as if I am oblivious to the very recent threat to my life.

I have no words just yet. We stand still, and he throws his arms around me. I give in to the embrace, and allow his strength and steely determination to comfort my weary body. I allow myself to be limp, as I give in to the need to feel connected to another. I hear a muffled sob from Daniel's mouth. His words follow. "You could have died."

I feel sorry for the pain I have caused my friend. I can't imagine what he is thinking right now. My arms find the strength to embrace him. "Thank you," I finally utter as I allow the tears to begin to flow.

Pulling back, he feels me return to him and places me at arm's length as he looks into my eyes. "We need to leave here. We need to go now." There is a very real desperation in his eyes I have not seen in him before.

"I know," I agree, but wonder what has made Daniel so frantic to run away.

"Let's grab your passport, and get to the airport. Let's leave tonight. We can take the first flight, and just go wherever we can."

I nod in agreement again. A plan is forming, and my energy increases as I imagine what else I might find important enough to throw into a backpack to take with me. I know I won't return to this ocean side paradise again – I can't possibly even if I wanted to. I have done too much damage as it is, to ever return here.

Daniel stares into my eyes. He acknowledges my agreement with a nod of his head and he drags me to the car. He isn't letting go of my wrist and I am grateful to him for doing so.

Daniel places me into the passenger seat. He retrieves a spare jacket from the back of his vehicle and throws it over me. My own clothes having been carried by the wind to the dark ocean below. My shoes, somewhere on the cliff top abandoned to be found by an avid photographer maybe. An eager soul who might one day too, risk the safety of the barrier to wander to the edge to snap the perfect photo. My bag and phone, their whereabouts are unknown to me. I have no recollection of where I have left them.

Daniel speeds in the direction of my rented house, eyes wide as he drives me to the safety of the little beach shack that has been my loved home for six months now. I should have known better. Six months was longer than I have stayed in any one location. The risk of being caught is too great to get comfortable in any one place for this amount of time, and to form such strong friendships. This is something I promised never to do. I had vowed never to let myself get so content that I would risk the lives of others. But yet, this is exactly what I had done in this place I currently call home.

I turn to look back at the smoke still billowing from Samuel's house. I will never forgive myself for allowing him to suffer in such a way - everything he owned, all the memorabilia; the records of his successful career now destroyed. All without reason or logic due to a stupid dalliance he enjoyed with a highly-strung romance writer. I will never ask for forgiveness, nor contact Samuel again, for doing so, would inevitably lead to his death. I am certain of this. Robert made me promise knowing that I care too deeply already for Samuel to do anything to jeopardise his safety.

I close my eyes and let the sadness overcome me. I have hurt innocent people here. I have caused all of this to happen. And why? To pretend to create a life I thought I was somehow entitled to? I will never forget this lesson I have been given. I will never risk another soul again. I look to my friend beside me and realise that I need to let him go too. I can't possibly risk his life by allowing him to run away with me. I could not live with myself if anything happened to this loving person who has begun to mean so much to me.

"Daniel…" I begin the delicate conversation. "I think I should go alone." I pause, waiting for his protest.

"No!" He answers firmly. "I'm coming. I am not letting you run away again. We are going together. You need me."

I am surprised at the firmness of his decision, his flamboyance and jocularity replaced with a directness and certainty that I haven't seen before. I know better than to argue with Daniel. He appears to have his mind set on coming with me. I allow the conversation to come to a natural end, and begin to formulate a new plan of escape that doesn't include risking my friend.

As soon as we arrive at my house, I begin immediately to pack a bag. The essentials are easy - my laptop, my camera, passport, credit cards and any cash on hand plus a few essential clothing items. Assuming I am continuing on my plan to land in Berlin, I focus on any warmer items I still have around. A pair of gloves, socks, essential traveller's boots that are comfortable, warm and waterproof. I look at my books and feel a sadness that they will be left behind. I search for my hard drive but can't easily find it. It is the one thing I tried to keep in a safe location and now can't remember exactly where that was.

"Daniel, I need to take a shower," I call as I turn to look at my friend who hasn't stopped checking the time, counting down the precious minutes I have so far taken to collect my possessions.

"OK, just hurry. There is a plane boarding in a couple of hours we might be able to catch but we need to get to the airport. I can't buy tickets online anymore, but once we get there we might be able to purchase them."

"Alright," I agree, quietly stepping into my bathroom. I put aside Daniel's jacket carefully, then discard my now quite unnecessary luxurious underwear. To think that when I dressed for the night, I imagined these same pieces of lace and ribbon to be removed by my sensual lover as we retreat for a night of passion. I was living in a dream imagining that somehow, I might have finally found my happily ever after - how did I fail so badly as to let my defenses and my strict security measures elude me?

As I step into the warm water of the shower, I allow the essence of the liquid to run over my naked skin. It is enticing, refreshing, and cleansing all at the same time. I feel the pleasure of the trickling of the shower run down my back as I begin to lather my hair with shampoo. My mind wanders between the practicalities of my escape alone and my desperate desire to see Samuel one last time before I leave. I wish I had the words to say to him to help him understand what I am about to do; to explain what I allowed to happen to him; to let him know that it was all my fault, and that he should always be vigilant for the word of a madman holds no weight. I tell him that the promises made under duress cannot be taken as gospel. That Robert may still be watching him and planning his next attack.

I won't let harm come to another person again. I won't let him risk himself for me. I apply the conditioner, and allow it to soak into my follicles as I soap my body. I feel the salt air purge from my skin. I will miss my ocean. I will miss this house. I feel a sudden sadness at what I am leaving behind. I have never felt this way before - never connected to a place as I have here but I knew this would be the case. I was drawn back here to my spiritual place one final time.

I felt the connection again from the moment I landed. I had pictured my beach, my ocean, the white sands and the crystal blue waters so many times in my head that I knew one day I would return. I couldn't have stayed away any longer, for I needed to replenish my soul with the waters from the beach that I call my secret beach, this home that I had known and loved so very much growing up all those years ago.

I knew this place held a special pull for me, which is why I imagine I stayed for so long, letting my defenses fall as I fell more and more in love with this ocean side paradise and its people.

Daniel pounds on the door. "Hurry up already!" he calls out to me. "If you don't come out I am coming in to get you." He threatens. I don't doubt him for a second. I know he has no shame when it comes to nakedness and he has complete comfort around me.

I still have no idea how I am going to sneak away from him. I wonder if I just have to let him come, and lose him at the first available opportunity once we are safely in Europe. That wouldn't be harsh at all. He would find his way around and probably meet some gorgeous stylish European men along his journey. And at least that means we don't have to have a massive dialogue about why he can't join me in my next destination. I resolve myself to let Daniel tag along until we at least get abroad. Somewhere in Italy I should think.

Leaving him alone in a country of sexy Italian men hardly seems a cruel thing to do at all. Daniel will probably thank me for it.

"Daniel? Can you find me something to wear on the plane?" I yell though the door as I rinse the last of the conditioner from my hair. He doesn't respond, surely still on his phone finding the flights to get us to our new destination. I step from the shower and wrap the towel around me. Looking in the mirror, I see for the first time the fatigue of the night's events in my face. My eyes are red from crying. My face is still slightly puffy and swollen from the injuries inflicted by my stalker. I look an absolute mess. I must remember to take some drops for my eyes on the plane. They are only likely to get more bloodshot the more I travel, they normally do.

"Daniel. Can you please pass me some clothes?" I repeat.

I am assuming he is just outside the door, ready for another warning knock to get me out and dressed. We do after all have to still drive by Daniel's house to pack a bag for him, so I figure I should get a move on.

With one towel carefully fastened around my breasts and another towel secured precariously around my wet hair, I open the sliding door of my bathroom to find some clothes. Instead I see Daniel standing in my room, his mouth slightly ajar. His expression is hard to place. "Didn't you hear me asking for clothes?" I wonder why he didn't answer if he was so close. He is most definitely within earshot and should have been able to hear me call his name.

He says nothing and just stands before me, perfectly mute. Then, out of the corner of my eye, there's another movement as the dark haired, black-eyed creature that is my stalker appears from the hallway and takes the few steps into my room, stopping just short of Daniel.

"Daniel, look out behind you!" I yell as I step forward to try to save my friend.

TWENTY-SIX

I lunge forward to reach Daniel, losing the towel around my hair in the process. I grab him, and try to pull him away from Robert who is just an arm's reach behind him, but Daniel is frozen in place, unable or unwilling to move from his position in the room.

I look into his eyes to try to register his current emotion. This must be what the involuntary freeze response looks like in a person - not able to move a muscle, not to be able to speak, not able to fight back to save oneself. Daniel is helpless. I cannot move him and I cannot seem to impart to him the current precarious nature of our situation.

Daniel has absolutely dissociated. My friend is present in body, but in body alone. He cannot communicate. He isn't hearing me. He is frozen in fear. He must have known my stalker was in the house. He must have seen or sensed him before I even stepped out from the bathroom.

"Daniel!" I scream at him, as I try to shake him awake from his frozen state.

Daniel just looks down at me, and shakes his head. I look behind him and see Robert is standing in place in my doorway. He is grinning from ear to ear as if he is pleased with himself. I don't know what he has done to Daniel, but I promise I won't let him hurt another person on my account.

"Stay away from him!" I yell at Robert. "Leave him alone. He has done nothing to hurt you. Just let him go. He isn't a part of this between you and I. Please just let him leave." I beg my stalker to spare the life of my friend.

He laughs as he takes the few steps to stand next to Daniel. "That's funny. That is what he asked of me too. He begged me to spare you. To let you get on that plane."

I look toward Daniel, and my heart drops from my chest, imagining him begging my stalker to save my life. I have underestimated the lengths Daniel would go to for me. I want to cry out to save him. I walk toward him and take his hands. I look into his eyes, and plead with him to come back to me. I beg for him to make a move, to help me to help save him. I can't bear to lose him now.

Robert begins to speak again. He is right beside Daniel now and he places his arm around Daniel as he speaks. "And I had to remind Daniel here that saving you was never part of the plan."

He lifts his hand, and turns Daniel's cheek so that their eyes meet. He presses his lips against Daniel, and kisses him. Daniel responds and moves his arms around Robert. The kiss is passionate and loving. It is familiar.

It all comes together, but slowly. "Daniel, you know him?" I ask, hoping that the answer I receive isn't the one I currently envisage.

And then, for some strange reason, I remember the tattoo. The design that I was sure was my very own - shared only with one other person, my plan to tattoo the yin and yang symbol in the shape of a wave. The position on my body was still to be determined but most likely my back. When I saw it on Daniel, I made a mental note to ask but never did. "Your tattoo?" I question the now silent Daniel.

Robert speaks on Daniel's behalf. "I thought you would surely recognise it, but you never asked. You never found out enough about the man you were fucking to find out how he had your very own tattoo design. Maybe if you hadn't been such a slut and actually took some time to get to ask some pertinent questions, you wouldn't be in this situation right now."

The bile rises in my throat, as I understand the true complexity of this plan. Daniel has been planted right under my nose to assist my ex-husband to manipulate and control me. I look at my friend. "Daniel?"

Daniel looks straight at me. "I'm sorry," he utters under his breath.

The hit to his face is swift and hard. The blood that flows from Daniel's nose is instant. And then another punch, followed by another. Daniel is barely able to stand up to the onslaught that is his punishment for daring to utter a word of sympathy for me in front of the man who has manipulated us both.

"You will not speak to her!" his punisher yells at him, kicking him to the ground.

"You are both to do exactly as I say." Robert screams at us.

He is losing it. My stalker is losing his self-control. How long has it been since he has had to raise his voice to me? Normally, he is so in control. Knowing and ordering every aspect of this terrorism, he has played the villain to perfection, right up to this point. He has Daniel in the exact position he wants him in - on the floor, cowering for his life, hands covering his face. His legs curled up in a ball, trying to protect his major organs as his lover kicks him repeatedly.

"Daniel, stay down!" I beg of my friend. I now understand that he too has been the victim of my cruel manipulator. Somehow, he has become a pawn in Robert's plan for murder. And Daniel played the role perfectly, something I will never forget. He forced himself into my life, into my bed. He allowed me to feel safe and to trust another person again.

Every aspect of the stalking over the last month runs through my mind, and I can see Daniel's part in all of it. He assisted Robert to be in more than one place at a time. The ease of access to my house, evident now as Daniel assisted Robert's entry. My friend and confidante Daniel, appearing at just the right time to rescue me, or to heal my wounds both emotional and physical. I recall the way my friend was undermining of my concerns, in front of police and with Shirley, obviously, trying to draw attention away from Robert's actions.

He planted the drugs in my house when I was unconscious, forcing ambulance officers to draw conclusions that were not true, further adding to the storyline that I was imagining everything happening to me. Constantly keeping me doubting every theory I had of the stalking. Every aspect of their actions together was an attempt to undermine my sanity.

Just then, I am forced to recall the day I arrived at Daniel's house - his bloodied face, the marks of strangulation imprinted on his throat. He too is a victim of this heartless and evil man. I cannot blame my friend for falling prey to the same madman that has tortured me for years.

"Stay down Daniel!" I scream at him, loud enough I hope to be heard over the sounds of Robert's boot pounding into Daniel's torso.

My ex has me in his sights now as he addresses me, exactly as I had hoped. I try to turn his anger toward me, for Daniel surely cannot survive much more of the brutality waged against him.

"You think you have any say about what happens here tonight?" Robert hisses at me.

And with those motivational words, I finally understand that I do. I do have control over what happens in this room today. I am going to control how this night ends. I am not going to die here today. This man is not going to end my life. I am going to fight.

As I ponder to formulate my next words in response to him, he knocks me to the ground. He kicks me over and over again, each contact causing what feels like an eruption in my stomach, my kidneys and my lungs. He kicks me until I want to pass out from the pain. He suddenly stops and looks at me.

"Is that how you want to play it…is it?"

He reaches down and grabs me by my throat. With his other hand, as support he pulls me up from the ground. My feet clamber to find their footing. I glance over to Daniel, still huddled on the ground, unable to move. Covering his face with his hands, pulling his legs into him in the fetal position. He will prove no more help to me today.

My ex-husband pins me to the wall and squeezes my throat, his favourite move. This is more like it. This is how I have always known he would try to end my life. I look him in the eyes. I will remain defiant until the very end. I will not give him the satisfaction of seeing fear in my face ever again. I will do this for Daniel. I will do this for Samuel. I will fight until I can't breathe anymore.

I kick out. I kick out and make contact. I see his eyes as he grimaces indicating that I have indeed hurt him. I grab at his arm, and dig my nails into the sensitive area above his veins on his wrist. I want to draw blood. I want to see him sense his own mortality before he takes my life. I dig deeper into his flesh, and with a sudden spurt of energy and clarity, I knee him in the groin. The result is instant, and he lets go of me as he doubles over in pain.

I run to the spot where Daniel lay on the ground. I hold him for a second as I beg him to leave. "Get up. Please. Get up and run!"

Robert's hand grabs a clump of my hair and pulls me backward onto the floor. I see the fear in Daniel's eyes as he watches me struggle with my attacker. I scream once more to him. "Run, Daniel, run!"

I am kicking into air. I am wasting energy struggling so I stop. I let my body go limp and I give into the next spate of pain. The adrenalin is racing through my body and my brain and I know I won't feel the real effects of this pain for days later. That is, if I get to live that long at all.

My ex brings his face down to meet mine. Through gritted teeth me warns me, "Stop with your games." He takes a moment to catch his breath. "Today, you will die."

"Fuck you!" I yell in his face.

He hits me again. It is sharp with a massive sting. I taste the blood in my mouth, and I am welcomed back to a world I know well - the split lip, the black eye, the blood streaming into my mouth. The taste gives me a reassurance I never knew I had. I have survived his attacks before. I know this position well. I will survive this one as well.

"Fuck you even harder!" I scream at him. He raises his hand once more to strike me, and stops himself mid-air. His brain is working overtime, thinking carefully about his next move.

"My lovely wifey has grown a set of balls I see," he sneers. "I appreciate that. I would like to think I have had something to do with that." He lets go of me and I scamper across the room to feel the support of the hard wall behind my back. It proves the only thing keeping me upright at this stage, for the chemicals that are allowing me to fight back are dissipating.

I am beginning to feel the ache of the most certain broken bones in my body. He is thoughtful. I can see the brilliant brain of his exploring a new idea.

"I will pay that my dear. You are after all, far more courageous than any of my other wives." He smiles as he lets me into his own world for just a moment. He doesn't want me to feel special. He now wants to attack the only weapon I have left, my confidence. "As a reward for your new-found strength, I will let you do it yourself."

I have no idea what this madman means by his statement. I feel vulnerable on the floor, so I try to stand. He immediately kicks my legs out from under me, and I land on the floor with a thump. He puts his face close to mine, and he spits his vile poison at me. "You will, my darling wife, take your own life."

He pulls a knife from a pocket on his belt. He holds it in front of my face as he begins to describe the end to my life as he envisions it.

"See this?" he asks, waving the knife in my face. He doesn't wait for a response. "Well, the vulnerable writer is going to end her own life. She is going to cut into her wrists. Just imagine it in the paper. It will be the most famous you have ever been. They will speak of the sad, pathetic, creative soul, like this was something, always destined to happen to her. The poor writer, alone and lonely with nothing but her imagined words as comfort finally killing herself."

I see him and hear his words, but don't accept any of it as my truth. There is no way this is how my life is going to end. I want to die in a small plane crash. I want to fall off a yacht while sailing and spend my last days drifting the open seas. I want to die a spectacular death under my own terms. Not like this. Not by this madman.

He lifts my hand to meet his and he places the knife into my palm. "Take this, and cut into the vein on your wrist. Cut downward."

I take the knife and immediately dig the sharp blade into my flesh. It stings as it delves further into the skin. I stop, and breathe the pain out. I take another breath in, and look him straight in the eyes as I cut away at my flesh. I dare not look at the blood as it starts to flow freely now from my forearm.

I smell the sweet scent of my own blood and know it well. He seems enticed by the scene, romanticised by the poetic justice he has finally served to me. He leans forward, and kisses my lips gently. "Goodbye, my wife." He says as he pulls his lips from mine. He believes this is my end, and in that second, I start to feel it too, as the blood drips now from my arm and onto my legs.

I am forced to look down, and see it. I feel weak but keep cutting, the pain now fully registering as the lifeline of blood leaves my body. I know I am going to faint, but I fight it for a while longer.

His face is close, smiling as he watches my eyes close for a second as I try to regain my senses. He puts his finger on my wrist, holds it there for just a second. The pressure feels comforting. He removes it, and moves his finger to his mouth to taste the sweet nectar of my blood on his lips.

Something catches my eye and I look up to see Daniel is behind him. Standing tall, his shoulders back, his chest pronounced. He looks at me for an instant, and I understand what his eyes tell me to do. He grabs Robert by the shoulders, pulling him backwards. The surprise in my ex-husband's eyes is evident as Daniel places his knee on his chest to hold him in place. He smashes a bottle into his face. The glass water bottle that had sat beside my bed is now imbedded in Robert's forehead.

My ex-husband struggles, but Daniel holds him in place a moment longer. He turns to me and screams "Use the knife!" I look at the knife in my bloodied hands, and understand what I am asked to do.

I get to my knees quickly, the blood covering my clothing, the floor and anything else I touch. I crawl the couple of steps to Daniel holding my ex on the floor. I reach up, and let my hand fall with the full force of my being. The knife pierces Robert's throat. I immediately pull it out and stab into the skin once more.

My heart is racing. I feel myself dying. I am losing so much blood. I don't think I can do anymore. I look to Daniel. "Keep going! It is him or us!" he begs, knowing that we have reached the point of no return. If we don't kill this madman now, we are both assured of a certain death.

I lose focus, so I stab into the unknown. My vision gets blurry, and I feel weakened with each and every stab into his flesh. I feel my blood mixing with his. Warm and sticky, the mixture of the two holds a scent that reaches my soul. I stab again and again. Daniel is silent. He has his job to do holding this madman in place. I suddenly lose sight of Daniel, and of the man who was once my husband.

I feel myself falling. With a thump, I hit the floor. I try to hold onto the knife, but it falls from my hand. My mouth fills with blood, and my mind goes blank as I feel the dark curtain of unconsciousness lower over my eyes.

TWENTY-SEVEN

"Daniel!" I yell into the darkness.

I can't see for the night has enveloped my vision. "Daniel!" I yell out once more. I hear footsteps, as Daniel makes his way across our small Italian apartment.

"I'm here." He whispers softly to me as he reaches out for me in the night. "I'm here. It is just a bad dream. Close your eyes my darling."

He crawls into the bed beside me and holds me tight. He strokes my hair knowing exactly how to get me back to sleep. "But Daniel…" I want to protest, to make sense of the visions of terror in my dreams.

"Shh, don't speak. It keeps you awake. Be silent. Close your eyes. I am here with you. We made it. Sleep now. Rest."

"I love you." I say to him as I close my eyes again. His strong arms lock around me holding me tightly.

"I tolerate you too my darling." He replies. I smile as I fall back to sleep.

* * *

Rome is alive with gorgeous men vying for my attention. Daniel is, at times, both intrigued and disgusted at the amount of attention an average looking blonde can attract in a foreign country. Long gone are the days of the disguises, and I'm back to my natural blonde locks. In good time too, I should imagine, as apparently Italian men love blonde women. A novelty for them, and one with a foreign accent as well is especially sought after.

Men will walk for blocks following us, giving us enough space to determine if Daniel is indeed my husband. But once his sexuality is established, the compliments come out, and Daniel steps aside to allow me to relish the attention of the attractive strangers.

"Why is it all about you here?" Daniel tries to understand.

"Men love Australian women. What can I say?" I tease him.

"Well what about Australian men?"

"We just need to find your people." I laugh as I taunt him.

"Fuck off." His temper is short when he isn't having regular sex, which means Daniel has to actually go out of his way to meet men to have sex. Not that having sex is a term that resonates with Daniel. He considers himself the ultimate lover and relishes the chance to brag of his skill in the bedroom.

"How is the book going?" Daniel asks.

"Finished" I am proud to announce.

"How?"

"Well, when you can't sleep, it opens up so much more time for writing. Not to mention the story began to write itself."

"So, do tell?" Daniel prompts me. "So, how does it end?"

"Happily, just as my readers would want. The bad guy gets what he deserves. The girl gets the guy. The guy gets the guy." I smile at how simple my synopsis will be to write.

"So, speaking of hot men, when is your actor boyfriend joining us?" He spits out the question as if the mere thought of Samuel's presence amongst us disgusts him.

"Daniel, you need to be nice. This will be the first time I have seen him since…" The words don't want to come readily from my mouth. I haven't seen Samuel since the night of the house fire. I never imagined I would again, but Daniel encouraged me to share my story with Samuel. And for that I will be eternally grateful. Since the threat of death from my ex-husband is no longer a concern, the possibility of a real relationship, the thought of an actual life to be enjoyed has become an exciting reality.

"I know." He says. Daniel is the one person who can understand the nightmare of my life and he doesn't make me finish my sentence. Having lived the nightmare himself with Robert, Daniel understands completely the very real risk to our lives that fateful night. He asks how I am feeling about seeing Samuel again.

"It's just we haven't been face to face since the fire and the night that Robert died." I take a breath as I say the words out loud. It still doesn't seem real to me, the idea that Daniel and I together ended a legacy of manipulation, abuse and murder.

How Daniel ever found the strength to fight back that night I still do not understand. A huddled-up ball on the carpet, he was unable to move until that one great force of strength and determination, which lead to my survival, and the death of the man who had hunted me down for years.

"It will be fine," Daniel assures me. "He understands, and doesn't blame you for any of it." He gives me a hug, quick and sweet. He doesn't want any of the surrounding available single men to assume we are a couple.

"So, you will make yourself scarce when he arrives, because you know it has been a while since we have…" I pause before finishing.

"Oh stop!" He puts his hands over his ears. "I don't want to hear anything about the needs of your vagina." He pulls a disgusted face as he says the final word. "Just go ahead and shag that hot actor boy. I just don't want to hear it from my room."

"OK, agreed!" I smile at him. "I will moan quietly so as not to disturb you."

"Enough about you. What about me? Where is my next delicious Italian meal coming from?" He pauses, and looks into the crowd of locals and tourists hurrying busily around the streets surrounding the Colosseum.

"How about that one? He looks very Roman to me." I point out a dark-haired stranger in the distance. A bag cradled to his side. A local I presume, surely off to a business meeting or working lunch. He is a designer maybe or creative soul by the looks of it. His attire is modern yet a little adventurous. He appears the perfect match for my artistic friend.

"Oh, he is nice. A bit on the young side, maybe." Daniel is fussy, and making every excuse imaginable to not face rejection, which means he chooses attractive, but not too attractive. He likes them youngish, but not young enough to reject him for being too old for their tastes. Daniel has a strict criterion for men and I have learnt it well.

I search the square. The traffic is slow, but haphazard in its direction, making sense to only locals themselves, or the few expats living abroad who have mastered the traffic system in Rome.

"Oh, he is cute!" I point out another man. Slightly older, sharing a laugh with a female companion, but very clearly gay due to his flamboyant mannerisms and obvious desire for attention.

"Oh, he's cute. I would do him!" Daniel exclaims.

"You would clearly do anyone right now. You are so desperate for it." I laugh at my own frivolity. I haven't felt this free for a long, long time, and I am getting used to laughing for the sake of laughing. Giggling at nothing in particular. Just laughing because I no longer have anything to be afraid of.

"Oh, very funny. Miss, I can't sleep with another man since I fell in love with some sexy actor."

"Yes." I can't argue that point. "Yes, I did fall in love and I am madly undeniably incredibly in love with Samuel! And I can't wait for him to arrive!" There I said it. These are the words I have wanted to say out loud ever since the moment I was able to make contact with Samuel again. The moment I knew for sure the threat against his life no longer existed.

I couldn't wait to explain it all to Samuel. I needed to tell him how very sorry I was for the fire that destroyed his home, for the loss of so many wonderful memories. I needed to explain to him the identity of the stranger he saw me kiss and how Max had managed to escape the fast burning fire that ravaged Samuel's home.

I had firstly to live up to my promise to Daniel to take him abroad, which I now feel I have adequately accomplished. Having explored Rome for the best part of a month, my time was now my own to meet Samuel once more and pick up where we left off, or so I had very much hoped we could do.

Only time will tell what happens for us next but at least we have a chance for a future that once would not have been possible.

And all thanks to Daniel and that brave moment that he stood up to fight back. I look to my friend once more sitting beside me in our favourite little café watching the world go by and of course searching the crowd for available attractive gay single men, which in Rome as we have learnt isn't all that difficult to find.

"Oh…there is one I could do."

Daniel points to a lonesome figure standing a street away. Meandering and seemingly lost for direction, his dark glasses cover most of his face, but his mannerisms somehow familiar to me. I stare a little longer at the stranger in the distance. He sees me too and removes his glasses. I see those dark soulless eyes, and I recognise him instantly.

"Daniel, no…no!" The fear registers immediately. I am barely able to stay seated as I recognise my ex-husband.

"I don't see him now," Daniel says, scanning the streets to try to locate the stalker in the distance. "Where has he gone?"

"Daniel, that is Robert! He is here!"

EPILOGUE

"Samara, darling, it's not him."

"Are you sure?" I beg Daniel for confirmation.

Daniel nods his head. There is a long silence before he speaks again. He clears his throat. "My therapist thinks you have Post Traumatic Stress Disorder. You know…that means seeing things that aren't really there. You see images from your memories but they feel real to you, because those images once were real."

I pause and consider the information honestly and realise Daniel isn't just talking about me as he describes the lapses in reality. "You see him too?"

"All the time." My friend admits. "In my nightmares. As I walk down the street. I see him out of the corner of my eye. I see his eyes staring at me in strangers. I think I see him as I turn a corner, hiding from sight but watching me. Always watching me."

I understand completely what Daniel is describing. The nightmares for both of us are so very real. "I still have visions of you huddled on that floor, frozen. I was scared that you would never move. I thought that was the last memory I would ever have of you. It still haunts me."

Daniel takes a large gulp of his wine before he speaks. "I can't stop seeing the blood. You covered in your own blood, it dripping down your arms and then his blood too. It was all over you, all over both of us. I can still smell it. The smell of it has never gone away." He pauses. The emotion in his voice is heightened.

"My therapist has talked to me about something else too my darling. Something I have been meaning to tell you."

I wait silently. Although I have yet to talk to a professional about what happened, I am intrigued by the reflections that Daniel does share from his sessions.

"It is something they call gaslighting."

I stay silent, waiting to hear more.

"It is when an abuser manipulates another to lead them to believe they are losing their mind." Daniel pauses, obviously heavy with emotion. "I did that to you. Robert and I both…we did that to you."

"Daniel stop, you don't have to say any more. We both know what happened but it doesn't matter anymore."

"It matters to me and I need to say it. Everything I did was to make you believe you were going crazy. To doubt everything that you knew was real. Ultimately if you couldn't yourself believe the attacks to be completely real then no one else would either. That meant police, Shirley, Samuel even. I did that to you."

Daniel looks directly at me. "I am so sorry."

I reach over and take my friend's hand. "Please don't tell me you are sorry ever again." He has said these words to me countless times. But I know now Daniel was as much a victim as I was. He had little control over what he was told to say and do. If he failed to perform just one task, he would surely have been punished. He was doing what he needed to do to stay alive. The control over and the power held by this one man in our lives was beyond imagination.

"But I am. You could have died that night Samara. You could have died and it would have been all my fault."

There is another long pause. The words on Daniel's mind need to be said. Finally said once and for all. "Samara, that night I found you on the point after Samuel's house burnt down, I knew I couldn't go through with it. I thought I was going to lose you on the cliff. I would never have forgiven myself if that was how you ended your life."

I lift Daniel's hand to my mouth and kiss the back of his fingers gently. "Shh, my darling. That was not your fault." I have thought about that night so often. Remembering now glimpses of the memories as they all start to come back to me slowly. New memories are returning each day now that I am safe again. I want my friend to know that he is not to blame for what happened to me.

"Daniel, I wasn't on that cliff thinking of killing myself. That's not what was happening."

"Then what?" He pleads for understanding from me. I have struggled to find the words in these, past few months to explain what happened that night.

"I just wanted to feel nothing. I wanted to free-fall through the air. I wanted to dive into the dark waters and feel free from it all. I needed an escape."

"You would have died Samara. You would have hit the rocks below and we would probably never have found you again."

"I know that now. I wasn't thinking. I was just running." I stop again to think about that fateful night. "I just wanted the pain of it all to stop."

"It's over now." Daniel promises me. "Even though it doesn't feel it yet. It's over. He isn't coming back."

I close my eyes hearing the words that I still can't fathom. My nightmare is over. The torment has ended. I can return to my spiritual home and my secret beach one day knowing that I can finally stop running from the shadows in the night.

Murderous Intent

ACKNOWLEDGEMENTS

This publishing journey was shared with family and friends, so that the end result is something I hope we can all feel a part of. I am truly honoured to have you all play an important role in the creation of this book with me.

My greatest love and a source of inspiration for me are my children. Blair and Connor, you lovingly taunt me about my endless editing and my storylines. Thank you for your creative visions and marketing guidance. Without you both, this book would not have found its way to publishing. I write stories in the hope to make some small change in the world and it is all due to my children.

Karen Cutler, you are an anchor that keeps me grounded and safe in rocky waters. How can I thank you for the hours of editing you generously provided? Your feedback and comments made this story come to life. You are an inspiration to me. This book belongs to both of us.

Nadine Meyn, my grammar and spelling guru, thank you for the endless days of correcting my mistakes. What a talent! You are a truly benevolent being. How did I get so lucky to have met you?

ACKNOWLEDGEMENTS

Val Wiseman, my favourite beta reader, you are always lending a helping hand, a thoughtful link, a friendly reminder that someone else in the world wants to see these stories come to life.

Melissa Spilstead, your insistence on alternate endings keeps me busy re-writing. You lead me to believe that I can do anything and I know I can with you by my side.

And to my heart, my soul, my inspiration, Mark Simmons. You are the first reader of everything I write. You encourage me and support me every single day. There is a little bit of you in everything I write. For this reason, you get the dedication on this novel. I hope it meets with your approval.

To the countless other family, friends, writers, authors and creatives who are too great in number to name individually. I thank you for your support, your strength, your encouragement and your continued belief in this crazy idea of mine to become an author.

Thank you!

Murderous Intent

www.ingramcontent.com/pod-product-compliance
Lightning Source LLC
Chambersburg PA
CBHW030626110726
47901CB00002B/339